2/18

D1521958

ALEXANDRIA RISING

A Novel

*To Glen,
Enjoy the journey!
Mr Walle Maguire*

Mark Wallace Maguire

Published by Speckled Leaf Press

Printed in the United States

ISBN: 1534815597
ISBN-13: 9781534815599

Special thanks to Steve Geyer and my family, near and far, for their encouragement. Thanks to Allen Bell, Paul Cantrell and Adam Miller.

This book is dedicated to my father, Jack, who taught me that reading for fun is just as important as reading for knowledge

PROLOGUE

The city stank.

It always stank in summer when the scents of the clogged drains, rotten food and sweating bodies combined for a noxious fog that hovered over its hills. Even the Thames stank, its shores lined with flotsam from forgotten ships, animal carcasses and mounds of refuse washed on the rising tides and left for the foragers from the sky and the beggars from the cracked cobbled streets.

But he ignored the stench. Stood at his windows opened defiantly, inhaled deeply, begging for a breeze to cool his beaten brow. Even a simple draft to flutter the tattered drapes would be welcome. Anything to soothe his fevered head, to alleviate the sweat bullets lining his chest, rivulets streaming down his arms, his legs.

He brushed a piece of lank hair from his forehead, sat down to his pockmarked desk, took another sip of watered-down wine and pressed the quill to the piece of parchment. His hand shaking, he pushed the words from his mind, half-muttering to himself as the black ink stained the yellow paper.

> *"The sight is dismal;*
> *And our affairs from England come too late:*
> *The ears are senseless that should give us hearing,"*

He took another deep breath, dipped the quill in the inkpot again. Started to write. Had to take a break. So hot. Leaned back his chair. A breeze? My soul for a breeze, he thought. Beneath his opened shirt, attached to a leather band, a sliver of translucent stone lay on his chest. It shifted colors in the half-light of the candle. Sometimes azure. Other times silver. A passing hue of cobalt. He clenched it. Inhaled again. Opened his eyes and grabbed the quill. Attacked the parchment.

> *"Let us haste to hear it,*
> *And call the noblest to the audience.*
> *For me, with sorrow I embrace my fortune."*

He leaned back again. Closed his eyes. Focused. Listened. Heard the sounds of the streets below. The usual calls of the pedestrians, the hawkers, the laughter of children, the occasional neigh of a horse or the bellow of a cow being led to slaughter. He heard clattering in the streets, the distinct sound of wagon wheels grinding on cobblestones, a sharp rapport.

He knew that they had come. Come for him. He was late. Again. But, there was so much perfection to do. So much to finish. So much yet to rewrite. But, his time was up. And he needed the money. The squeak of a carriage door, he could even hear the footfalls, knew it was him. The benefactor. Then the words shouted above the din of the crowd.

"William!"

He ignored it. Clutched the stone in one fist. Gulped down the last of the drink with the other. And began writing again, the thoughts racing now, he had to force himself to slow down, lest the writing be unreadable. The shout again from the streets.

"William! Where is it? I need it now. I am coming up and Martin is coming with me. I know you're there. They told me you were at home at The Fox and The Hound. I see your window is open. Unlock your door."

He knew he could no longer wait. It was time. He wrote quickly. Dipped the quill in the inkwell for a final push and then finished the last few lines.

*"The soldiers' music and the rites of war
Speak loudly for him.
Take up the bodies: such a sight as this
Becomes the field, but here shows much amiss.
Go, bid the soldiers shoot."*

Heavy thud of big boots on the worn wooden stairs. A knock at the door. He scribbled a title on the first page. Blew on the ink. Rolled up the parchment, wrapped a ribbon around it. Took the chain from around his neck. Lifted the lid of a wooden box on his desk. Dropped it in. Cinched up his shirt. Lumbered to the door. Opened it.

"Is it ready?"

"Of course, I was just taking a nap."

The man snatched the roll from his hands. Slid off the ribbon, opened it up. Read the first few lines.

"A nap….Mmmmmm," a low groan, then, "Interesting opening. I like ghosts. Audiences love ghosts. A good start."

"Here," the playwright said. "Flip to Act III, yes, there a few lines down."

The man did so, patiently, eyes intent.

Then reading. The lines of angst giving way to surprise, then relief. A smile.

"Late as usual old friend, but it looks good. By Jove, I do love these lines here in this act. My God. Very powerful. The very sense of the universe itself isn't it? The only thing I don't like so far is the title. Usually you're very succinct on these, but it looks like this was an afterthought, 'Hamlet.' It could be a play about a small village and that wouldn't draw the crowds would it?"

The playwright ran a hand through his hair. His mind still reeling.

"How about, 'The Tragedy of Hamlet, The Prince of Denmark'? Yes, a bit more detail. Will that work?"

The man looked at him. Peered deep into his eyes. The playwright answered his own question.

"Yes. That's it. 'The Tragedy of Hamlet, The Prince of Denmark.' By William Shakespeare."

The man shook his head, let forth a small chuckle.

"It is a bit wordy, like I have a mouthful of stones, but it will work. And I am sure once people see it, they'll remember it. I don't see how you do it and keep doing it. You may be late, but you're good son. You are good. Time may forget you, but I won't."

"Time forgets us all, my friend, but for some it takes longer than others."

CHAPTER ONE

Present Day
Atlanta, Georgia

The rain fell in thin, erratic sheets, alternating its direction according to the whims of a once-strong hurricane that had hit Florida two days before and whose remains now sputtered over Atlanta, like the last soldiers of a once-great army determined to deliver the remnants of its once fierce power upon the land.

Rand O'Neal stood at the front of a sizeable black-clad crowd gathered in Oakland Cemetery. As Atlanta's oldest graveyard, it was not only a historical site but an unplanned salute to the oxymoronic nature of the city itself – ancient, mildewed tombstones, ornate mausoleums and stately oak trees sat under the nearby visage of glittering skyscrapers. Old Atlanta families lay buried here and new Atlanta families visited it for pleasure.

Rand had one hand thrust into a pocket where he crumpled the bulletin from the funeral, the other hand was tucked under his grandmother's arm, supporting her usual stoic facade now on the verge of crumbling. They watched as his grandfather's coffin was lowered into the ground. The neatly dug rectangle swallowing the body of Henry O'Neal, one of the pillars of the South's academic scene.

The minister's voice carried on, his words now ceaseless static to Rand. He stared up at the shifting sky, watched the sweeping storm clouds moving fast, felt the patter of rain on his face. Such a cliché he thought. A funeral. With rain. He smiled inwardly at his own joke. Always finding humor, even in death. The feigned jokes, the odd analysis, the easy jabs always a friend at his side, a defense mechanism he had used to fight off the black demons that encroached his soul since his own parents had died years before.

"A-Men." The minister proclaimed.

"A-Men," the crowd mumbled back. Rand felt his grandmother's arm lower, her hand squeeze his. He squeezed back and planted a gentle kiss on her cheek. There were no words to say. Rand would not deliver empty platitudes here. He knew his grandfather would not have approved. What was done, was done. So he said nothing. Just stood. Feet frozen.

The well-wishers began filing toward them. But Rand had been inundated with condolences the last few days. Since his grandfather had died three days before, he had spent every moment at his grandparents' house where he helped fill the void of the empty halls and play host to the endless procession of guests at their door. The friends, the distant aunts and cousins, the colleagues from Emory University. The church members. The Rotary Club members. And the telephone calls. And drop-ins. He was tired. Immune to the words. Tired of heavy hugs from perfume-laden ladies and numb to firm handshakes from stone-faced men. The lack of sleep, the numbness had caught up with him. Someone had half-joked that his bloodshot green eyes looked like Christmas. He didn't laugh.

He glanced behind him, saw a family friend, motioned for her to come up, then leaned over and whispered in his grandmother's ear.

"I need some space. I'm feeling a little faint. Miss Louise will stay here with you, okay?"

He would've felt guilty, but he had devoted the last three days to be by her side and had not left her home.

He knew she would understand.

She turned and smiled at him.

"Of course, my boy. You've done us all proud. Go take a walk. Me and Louise will be fine right here."

"I'll meet you back at the car."

Rand walked in the other direction of the crowd, head bent, eyes focused on the ground. He could find a quiet place, then double-back to the car. He reached in his pocket for a cigarette. Remembered he had quit smoking. Muttered a curse under his breath.

"O'Neal!" a half-shout from behind him. He recognized the voice.

It was Adam Scott, the sports editor at the newspaper where he worked and a friend from his days in high school when the two of them played defense on the football team. The bear of a man was half-jogging toward him, his belly heaving, his snug pants straining against his thighs.

"Damn Adam, I didn't recognize you with a tie on. And your hair brushed. And shaven. And, well, totally not looking like shit."

Adam smiled.

"Glad you've still got your humor about you." He clasped a beefy hand on Rand's shoulder, the two walking amid the listing tombstones.

"Yeah."

"I called you, like four times…"

"Yeah, I saw. I've been busy. I haven't answered the phone. I quit answering my phone. Everyone called. I had to stay on my toes just to answer my grandmother's phone and door so I quit. Turned the damn thing off. Let the battery die."

Adam laughed.

"I've never known anyone who hates talking on the phone as much as you."

"Damn nuisance. My ear hurts. You can't read people's body language. Terrible."

"And, yet, you spend most of your time at the paper on the phone."

"But there's the rub, my friend."

"What's that?"

"There I get paid to be on the phone."

They walked in silence. Rand cast a glance back to the thinning crowd by the grave, his grandmother still standing there like an oak tree in the wind. Strong. Stolid.

"You all right, man?" Adam asked.

"Yeah, just tired. Beat. They had a wake last night at the Hibernian Society. I didn't stay too late, but late enough. Too many Guinness, but nothing a couple of Advil and Gatorade won't cure."

"Only one wake?"

"No, I've got another one at the Firefighter's Association tonight and then God knows what else. A reception at Emory later this week. Everybody wants to send out Henry O'Neal with a blast and as the only surviving male relative, well, they figure I'm the one to do all the drinking."

"Worse things could happen. You need company?"

Rand laughed at the joke. Then stopped mid-stride.

"You know, actually I could. I am tired of the small talk, nodding at the stories. Yeah, I could use company. Can you call in sick? Pick me up around 7? I'll be at my grandmother's again, at least for a few more nights before returning to my shack in Smyrna."

CHAPTER TWO

H is head hurt. And the voices from the radio made it worse.

"That's right, Atlanta. We've got another hot one. Summer is here and the heat is with it. Hope everyone enjoyed that cool spell, because it will be a while before we see that weather again."

"You said it, Bob. Look for a high of 94 today with a chance of thunderstorms this afternoon. Enjoy the sun, but don't forget that umbrella."

94 degrees.

Damn.

The air conditioning had coughed out its final breaths two days ago. Now, he was living on a window unit and a house full of fans. The shotgun house he rented in Smyrna was barely up to code and he knew getting the A/C fixed could take up to a week with his stingy landlord.

The strains of a post-modern pop anthem began blaring from the radio. Some faded version of U2. The jangly guitars. The echo upon echoes.

He leaned over and slammed his hand into the clock radio, silencing the music. Read the numbers blaring back at him.

8:14 a.m.

Damn.

He had a zoning meeting at 9 he had to make. Some article on residents complaining about a new shopping center near their neighborhood. He knew the drill. Get the vote on the outcome. Ask city council if they would approve it, get residents' reactions and a quote from the developer. He already had the statistics on the development emailed over earlier in the week - parking spaces, abatements. Anchor tenants, tree ordinance. He could do it practically in his sleep. He knew he could do it hungover. And that was good, because hungover he was. He had spent another late night at Rosses Point Pub, his favorite and now-regular after work haunt. Sometimes he would drink with friends after work, sometimes a group of colleagues from the newspaper and sometimes, like last night, alone.

He brewed a pot of coffee. Washed down a couple of Advil with the first cup, took a shower, dressed and slid into his Camry to drive to city hall.

8:57 a.m.

He would be a little late, but these things could go on for hours. He would have most of it written in his head before the meeting was even halfway over.

CHAPTER THREE

"Good story, O'Neal." The voice came from a news editor whose only presence in the newsroom was a set of overgrown eyebrows and a shiny bald head always hovering behind a huge monitor.

"Thanks. I shot you over a sidebar too with some bullet points if you want it."

"Saw that. We'll give it a look."

Rand leaned back in his chair and guzzled another Gatorade, waiting for the hydration to saturate his brain and body again, the Advil beginning to wear off now. The night before creeping back with its punishment.

"Well, there's the new spokesman for Gatorade's marketing campaign. Woodward, Bernstein and

O'Neal! Serious thirst quencher for serious journalists!"

The voice behind him boomed. Adam had just walked in for his shift on the night beat.

Rand recognized Adam's jab at their continual debate on if he was, in fact, "a serious newspaperman" or not. Rand had explained repeatedly that, yes, he worked at a newspaper. And yes, he was a good writer, but he was not a journalist. Graduating college armed with an English degree and a penchant for being a smart ass, he had little direction. His grandfather had offered to make phone calls for him, introduce him to connections, to, frankly, get him a job. Rand was not interested. He didn't want to be like the soft, legacy kids he had grown to loathe. The kids whose reputation was built on Southern Company and Coca-Cola stock. The kids who went to private schools, got into the colleges of their choice on donations and last names. Nope, Rand was determined to be different. He wanted to earn what he had. He shunned any attempts by his grandfather to get him to attend private school and attended public school in the Atlanta suburb of Decatur where he played outside linebacker on the football team with Adam, the only two white players on the state's best defense.

When college rolled around, he had been invited to apply for Harvard and Yale, but only because of his last name. Instead, he attended a small liberal arts college in Virginia. He had only stumbled into the newspaper business because Adam had asked him to come work there after the senior political reporter had quit on a whim during election season. Rand had been working at a coffee shop for a few years, dishing out espresso with quips when Adam dropped in. Rand cited his lack of experience, but Adam had begged him to come in for an interview. "They're desperate," he had said. "It's election season. They need anyone, just someone who can fog up a mirror. You can out write anyone I know in your sleep. News should be easy. Just show up sober and shaven and tally election results for a few weeks. If nothing else, it's better than serving coffee."

That was four years ago. Rand had not only survived that tumultuous election season, but had thrived. The pace, the thrill of deadlines, the pressure tapped into his competitive personality. The writing itself came easy. Adam had not lied. Now, he was the best reporter in the newsroom, though he still volunteered to anyone who would listen that he was not a reporter. Just a writer. Hired as a mercenary. Despite the awards, the top articles assigned for 1A and the clichés of drinking too much and a habit for not ironing, he was not a journalist.

CHAPTER FOUR

The files upon files of papers in his grandfather's study were overwhelming. Even with Atlanta's top legal duo 'Haskins & Hall' and his grandmother's insight into the mish-mashed filing system, Rand's head was swimming. They had met to read the will. The will made sure that Rand's grandmother would be taken care of. A handful of charities would have early Christmas gifts. For Rand? His grandfather had left him his car, an older model boat of a Buick, his books and collections of bric-a-brac. Rand was also left in charge of sorting through the barrage of academic documents in his grandfather's home study - the research, the family history, the inconsistent attempts at memoirs and a dozen other mounds of minutiae that ranged from decades-old pay stubs to countless letters.

There would be more specifics to come on the money in time, the lawyers told them. Henry O'Neal had left the details of his finances and stocks stored in several safety deposit boxes in one of Atlanta's oldest banks.

"But with access and time, we will sort that out and meet here again. Unfortunately, with a mind as complex as Henry's, these things take more time than usual," assured Jack Hall, senior partner at the firm.

By late evening, Rand had made a small dent in the piles. The lawyers had only stuck around long enough to sift through a few file folders for any forgotten documents and his grandmother had been quickly overwhelmed by the memories, leaving the study after only half an hour, feigning a headache. Now, in the fading wake of the lawyer's cologne, Rand sat alone at the old wooden desk, an open bottle of wine to keep him company. He had placed his grandfather's favorite record on the record player and the easeful sounds of Vivaldi's mandolin and cello concertos hummed softly. Soon, he was asleep.

CHAPTER FIVE

"Thank God it's Friday," Rand announced to the newsroom.

No one paid him attention. Ears welded to phones. The police scanner spitting static. Questions sailing back and forth between reporters and editors.

Rand leaned back in his chair, chewed on a pencil. Studied the screen in front of him. Did a Google news search on breaking news. Localized it to North Atlanta.

Dunwoody woman spots fox in her yard
Wreck on Interstate injures four
MAKING WAVES: Atlanta swimmer tries out for Olympic team

Nothing. Clichéd headlines. Commonplace stories. Same old, same old. He opened his other windows. Bloomberg. WIRED. ESPN. Checked the stock market. Outside of the international markets, it was status quo.

"Rand, what you got for me today?"

Shit, the news editor had spotted him over the sea of cubicles.

"Ah, working on something right now, boss. I've got a follow up piece from last night on the new health insurance benefits for city employees and, I'm working on something else right now…did you know that Chinese Tech stocks jumped this morning with announcement of a software merger? Maybe we could localize that? Talk to some university professors, hedge fund managers…"

"Our readers don't give a damn about the Chinese stock market. They want local news. Local faces. Come up with something else. But back to this benefits story? What's the angle?"

"Ah, just basic stuff. Ironing out of the details. Picking a provider. The mayor is grandstanding right now, but the real question is who they will choose. The mayor's brother is on the board of the state's largest health provider so I think he'll go with them. Typical cronyism, though you won't let me call it that. Anyway, should be about 500 words. No new photos. We can just use headshots."

"Good. I need it by 4 today. And try to get me a second story for us to run this weekend. Nothing time sensitive, just something so I don't have to fill up 1B with AP material again. The publisher chewed my ass about that yesterday, okay?"

"Yes sir."

Rand slunk in his chair. He had already written most of the benefits story and just needed to plug a fresh quote. He hoped he could sleepwalk through the rest of the afternoon and duck out early for a pint. But, now, he needed to find another story. He opened his email inbox and began scanning for ideas.

CHAPTER SIX

"You have a visitor in the lobby, Mr. O'Neal."
The voice purred through the phone.

"Thank you, Sarah. And please, just call me Rand."

"Yes, Rand."

It was a game they played every time he had a phone call. The voluptuous receptionist Sarah Smith and Rand. She liked to call him, 'Mr. O'Neal' for some reason and he always had to remind her it was, "Rand." Which she enjoyed. She was a cute, slightly overweight divorcee who was born with a mouth made for mischevity. Rand never took their flirting beyond a smile or a wink, but knew she enjoyed the attention. And, honestly, he did as well.

In the lobby stood Jack Hall. He was dressed for summer in the quintessential Southern gentleman's outfit de rigeur of a seersucker suit and a smart bow tie.

"Hello, Rand."

"Hey, Mr. Hall. How are you? What brings you to our illustrious institution?" he said, shaking the outstretched hand.

"I'm fine, thanks. I tried your cell phone a few times this morning, but it went straight to voice mail so I decided to drop by and deliver this in person; I had a meeting up here with Judge Morrell," he said, extending a thin manila envelope to Rand.

"Oh, sorry about the phone. The battery died last night and I haven't had time to recharge it. I've been busy here all day trying to find a story for tomorrow's paper that will get my editor off my back. Sorry you had to stop by."

Hall gave him a terse smile.

Rand took the envelope, light in his hands.

"I don't know what's in it, Rand. It was sealed, of course, so I didn't open it. But we discovered it early this morning when we finally unlocked the first box. This was at the top of the stack," a wan smile accompanied the remark.

"I understand about that," Rand said. "I've been going over to my grandmother's the last two nights and staying up way too late trying to sort out his papers. The man definitely believed in the power of paper. He loved trees, but he didn't love trees, I guess you could say..."

The wan smile again.

"Well, I must be on my way. Good luck on finding that story for your editor."

CHAPTER SEVEN

"*For Rand.*"
His name was scrawled on the front, his grandfather's handwriting pushed from one of his old fountain pens. The back of it was sealed with wax, his family's coat of arms stamped into it, one of the old traditions his grandfather had clung to, "anything that separates us from the animals, even if the rituals do seem useless, they stand for something," he had often confided.

Rand lay it on the desk. Studied it. There nothing nefarious. Nothing out of the ordinary. Stared at it some more, tuning out the Friday afternoon buzz of the newsroom.

He gently shook out the contents spilling onto his messy desk.

A small brass key fell out. Then, a slip of paper. It was on bank letterhead, tiny indentations from a typewriter pierced its thick surface.

SkyTRUST Atlanta
1756 Peachtree St.
Atlanta, Ga.
Serving Georgia for over 200 years

Safe Deposit Box: 232377
Rand O'Neal

Rand was confused. Had his grandfather been keeping something for him? Maybe something from his parents? Maybe something from the will he didn't want taxed? He gingerly put the contents back in the envelope. Lifted his briefcase from the floor, another relic of his grandfather's, slipped the envelope in. Sat. Thought.

"Hey boss, I think I got that second piece. I just got a lead on a heartwarming feature about a Russian immigrant who is going to college on a scholarship. I'm going to run out and try to track it down," he lied.

"Track it down? Run out? You got a phone number or confirmation? Is it a state college? Are taxpayers funding this scholarship? What's the school board say?" The bushy eyebrows didn't move.

"I'm having issues with that, so, er, I am going to go over to her parent's apartment and try to talk to her mom. I should be back later. Should be a winner though."

Rand took the silence as acquiescence, didn't wait for an answer, grabbed his briefcase and drove to the bank.

CHAPTER EIGHT

The knocking at the door would not stop.

Rand cracked an eyelid, its weight crushing and saw the red-eyed clock radio staring back: 10:21 a.m.

It was Saturday. He wasn't working. Why was someone banging at his door?

"Hold up!" he yelled through a parched throat. "I'm coming!"

He yanked a pair of dirty khakis off the floor, threw on a clean T-shirt and splashed water onto his face. On the sink sat the bottle of Advil. The now familiar cure for late nights of too much drinking. He emptied four into his hand and tossed them back.

The knocking started again.

"I'm coming! Hold your damn horses!"

He figured it couldn't be too important. It could wait a minute longer. If it was the police, they would've have identified themselves as such. If it was an emergency from a relative or friend, they could've come around to his back door. It was probably a relentless Jehovah's Witness or someone to finally repair his air conditioning.

In the kitchen was the remnants of yesterday's coffee, sitting thick and bitter. He poured it into a dirty mug, heated it in the microwave, extracted it with tentative caution, then slumped across the den and cracked open the front door.

A crisp grey suit, white pressed dress shirt, no tie met him.

Head clean shaven. No trace of stubble on his white cheeks. Deep black eyes.

He was tall, but not too tall, Rand himself coming in just under six foot three, the slight paunch still not betraying his athletic past.

"Yes," he offered lifting the cup to his face slowly slurping in the elixir.

"Mr. O'Neal, may I come in?" the voice was delivered flat. Rand thought he detected a slight accent, - English, Welsh perhaps?

Rand eyed him. Lifted the cup of coffee to his lips again. Studied the situation.

"I would welcome you in, but who are you and, not to be acerbic, what do you want?"

A slight smile crossed tight lips.

"It is a long story, one to be better discussed sitting down or," then motioning to Rand's cup, "over coffee."

"With all due respect, I need a little more than that," Rand said. "Sorry, I'm not going to invite just anyone into my house without some identification or explanation. I've got a 9 millimeter on me and I am not afraid to use it," he lied.

Rand had never owned a gun in his life, though he did have a smart collection of pocket knives in his closet and a baseball bat leaning behind the door.

"Of course, of course. Apologies." The man at the door set his briefcase down and reached into his pocket. He withdrew a small business card. A plain white simple matte.

Mark Venator
Aeolus Industries
London Athens Salzburg New York

Rand turned it over. There was nothing else. No phone number, website or address. He felt the man's eyes studying his face.

"Okay," Rand took another long sip of coffee, the Advil and caffeine burning a hole in his stomach.

"Now I know who you are Mr. Venator, but what do you want?"

"I am here to discuss your late grandfather's estate. There are a few items that weren't in the will I need to wrap up on behalf of my company."

"I thought everything was handled. Are you affiliated with Haskins & Hall?"

"No, not exactly with that firm, but, rather, shall we say affiliated with your grandfather's work."

Rand paused. Urged his brain to work. Tried to force himself to wake up.

"Can this wait? I worked yesterday and then had a rather late night. Plus, all of my grandfather's papers and research are either at his home or at Emory. I don't have access to any of his papers at the moment. My grandmother and the attorneys are handling all the legal work with his will. Candidly, I don't think I can help you right now."

"Actually, you can help us now. I just need a few minutes of your time."

"How about we meet around dinner tonight or sometime tomorrow?"

"I am terribly sorry Mr. O'Neal, but my company wants me to handle this as soon as possible," Venator looked at his watch as if to emphasize the point. "It is of the utmost importance to our interests."

What the hell? Rand thought, but his curiosity overcame his tentativeness and he opened the door all the way, "Okay, come in. Excuse this mess, this chaos. I had a few friends over, we had a late night and –"

"That is okay," Venator interrupted, "I remember what it is like to be young and carefree."

Rand nodded, picked a pile of books off a chair and offered Venator a seat. He sat across from him on the couch, a rickety coffee table between them filled with several empty beer bottles, a tattered notebook and a scattering of newspapers. Rand was less wary, but still on guard. He still didn't know if this guy was with law enforcement, NSA, or CIA. And Aeolus – wasn't that Greek or Roman? – Industries. He remembered a half-memory of the word from somewhere in his studies.

"Can I get you a cup of coffee? Yesterday's goodness. Just a minute to re-heat."

"No thanks," again the tight smile. "This shouldn't take longer than a few minutes."

Venator set the briefcase on the floor, unlocked it and lifted a small envelope that he flipped open with an immaculately groomed fingernail.

"Very good then. Here is where we stand. Mr. O'Neal, I believe you were recently provided with a key to a safe deposit box, correct." A statement, not a question. "According to our records, the box was accessed yesterday close to 3 p.m. Did you retrieve the contents of the box and, if so, have you had an opportunity to go through it?"

"Uh, yes, I did retrieve it, but, no, actually, I haven't had the chance to look through it," Rand said. Damn. Damn. Damn. How had he forgotten about the small gleaming wood box that was tucked inside the safe deposit box? He had accessed it Friday, but the box had stayed tucked in his brief-case throughout the rest of the day and into the night when he and Adam had invaded Rosses Point Pub and worked hard at decimating their supply of Guinness. Eventually, when reason started to fade and wallets grew thin, a cooler head prevailed and they went to Rand's home.

Rand recalled carelessly tossing his briefcase into his bedroom closet. In the rush and the blur of night, it was the last thing on his mind. He wanted to be in a good place – physically and mentally – before peering into it. He needed a break from the ever-present ghost of Henry O'Neal and he figured any more ventures into the past he wanted to tackle clearheaded, sober and in solitude.

"But, how do you know about – "

"Never mind that, Mr. O'Neal. The question is, A) Do you still have it and, B) How much are you willing to sell it to us for?"

"Uh, I believe I still have it."

"Mr. O'Neal, please," the tight smile spread into a full grin. "Belief is assigned to demons and angels. You either have it or you do not and considering the fact that none of your friends left with it last evening, I assume it is still in your possession."

Even the fresh caffeine swimming to Rand's brain was not enough to test the fathom of this man's words. Belief? Selling it? How does he know I have it? Friends leaving with it last evening?

Seemingly reading his mind, Venator said: "Well? Let's not beat around the bush as you Americans like to say. How much are you willing to part with it for? My company is willing to offer $100,000. Tax-free, of course. Cash. No questions asked."

Venator must've read the confusion on Rand's face so he continued, his voice dropping an octave, a sickly sweet persuasive tone, "That's right Mr. O'Neal. $100,000. That's over three times a year what you make now. Granted you will get a nice settlement from your grandfather's estate when your grandmother dies, but how about now? Why, you could buy a new car. A house. Take an extended vacation in Italy, Thailand or even Ireland again."

The "again" was what grabbed Rand's attention. Something was wrong. Very wrong. This man knew too much. Not only of the present, but of the past. Rand had visited Ireland many times with his grandfather, but had not been to the Emerald Isle in over six years.

Rand's mind began working. Play dumb. Play dumb. Play dumb.

"Hmmmm…let me think about it."

A pinch of irritation in the eerie collectiveness of the man's eyes.

"Okay, $200,000."

"Hmm….how about this Mr. Venator? Let me brew a fresh pot of coffee, shower and think about it. Then we can meet for dinner and make a deal."

"We cannot wait until dinner. I have a plane leaving in a few hours. We need the box immediately."

Again, Rand detected increasing irritation in the man's voice.

Who are "we?" Rand wondered.

"Okay, how about this then. Let me clean up and shake these cobwebs out of my head. I had a late night, like you said," Rand managed a grin. "Then, say, let's meet again in about an hour – " he glanced at the clock on the wall. "How about noon at, let's see, at Chesney's Coffee shop, just around the corner – you probably drove past it – and wrap it up….I just need a little time to wake up. As you can tell, I'm not a morning person."

The man's lips pursed, but, his eyes remained cool. Rand felt an immediate tightening of the air around him. A type of animal tension between the two of them.

"Very well, then," the man said. "But we won't do much more negotiating than over our current price. $200,000 is an extraordinary amount. That said, one hour. 11:30. I will see you then."

"Thanks," Rand exhaled, even though he did not know why he was thanking him. For some reason he felt indebted to the man for providing him the extra time after the tense exchange.

"Of course, Mr. O'Neal. I understand. Such decisions must be weighed on with a clear head." The tight-lipped smile again.

Rand ushered him to the door and watched him walk toward the street where a new silver Mercedes sat with the engine humming. The windows were tinted so he could not see if there were additional passengers in the vehicle.

The car silently glided away on shiny rims and polished wheels. Rand could not make out the license plate. Damn. That would have helped. He could have someone at the paper run it and figure out what in God's name was going on.

Across the street he saw his neighbor, the ever-present Mrs. Brown and her poodle on her front porch watching the scene. With her insatiable curiosity and penchant for gossip, he knew she would be at his door within the hour. He knew he would ignore her knocks as he had done many times be-fore. He did not have time for idle talk.

The coffee growing colder in his hand, his mind began to spin.

CHAPTER NINE

One hour.

$200,000.

Something wasn't right and Rand knew it. He had been blessed with strong instincts – a quality that, in part, had given rise to his ascension in the newsroom– and he knew something was amiss.

Why would that box be worth so much?

What could be in it?

$200,000?

Though Rand had shunned most of the upper-class trappings that came with his grandparents' status in the Atlanta community, it was challenging to shun all of the lure of not worrying about money.

Rand wasn't poor, but was barely breaking even raking in a paltry $550 a week.

He thought of the number again.

$200,000.

He couldn't wrap his mind around it. He did know one thing. He didn't feel safe. He felt watched. The man who came to the door knew too much. The bank visit. His friends. His grandfather. His background. His head was still aching from the night before, but he had the urge to leave. He told himself he was being paranoid. That he had watched too many spy movies and read too many Robert Ludlum novels, but damn it, better to be safe than sorry. He walked into the bathroom, closed the blinds. Turned on the faucet, ran the water over his face again. Stared into the mirror. The face stared back. No revelations greeted him. He was here. He was awake. There was no doubt. He slathered on deodorant and cologne to cover any leftover scents of beer seeping through his pores. In his closet, he slipped an ironed blue dress shirt over his T-shirt he hastily tucked into the khakis. Donned an old Braves baseball cap. In the back of the closet, half-hidden in the darkness, leaned the briefcase from where he had unceremoniously dropped it. He unclasped it. Retrieved the wooden box inside, stuffed it, a notebook and his cell phone into an old backpack not used since a hiking trip years before. The briefcase he left on the floor of the closet. He turned on his stereo, locked his front door and then slipped out his back door.

CHAPTER TEN

"**D**amnit!"
The voice echoed across the floor of Rosses Point Pub.

"Sorry, terribly, sorry," Rand apologized to the handful of patrons hunched over their pre-noon drinks and sandwiches. Not that anyone cared, but old habits die hard and he could imagine his grandfather chastising him for using such language in public.

He had uttered the phrase when he noticed his cell phone battery was dead.

He held his head in his hands, felt the sweat trickling down his forehead. He was hot, too hot to even enjoy the pub's famous black coffee. Instead he lifted a glass of ice water to his head and closed his eyes.

Tried to think. After he left his house, Rand had eased into the canopied protection of a yawning park just behind his home. He found a familiar path that ended just a couple of blocks from Rosses Point Pub. He had forged through the June heat, hoping to gain some half-seclusion, some illumination and make some phone calls before his meeting at 11:30.

"Art," he called out across the bar.

"Yeah," the grizzled bartender turned to greet him.

"Mind if I use the house phone? My cell phone is dead again and I really need to call someone."

"Dead, again, huh? I don't even know why you have that thing. But, yeah, go ahead."

Art Mulligan, whose all-too-familiar response was always, 'yeah' reached underneath the bar and eased out an old rotary style phone that once must had been white, but through years of use, cigarette smoke and spilled drinks was now a dank yellow.

"Thank you, sir." Rand picked it up, plugged his fingers into the dirty circles, winding each number, the old rotary heralding flashbacks of his 80s childhood. Unlike most people in the cell phone era, he had actually memorized several cell phone numbers, a practice from the days of his holdout as the last of the pay phone users.

He tried Adam.

The phone went straight to voicemail.

"Hello," the greeting said. "I'm not available. You know the drill."

"Hey, it's O'Neal. Listen, man. I need to talk to you ASAP. There is some weird shit happening right now...strange things afoot. My phone's dead and I don't have a charger, so, I don't know...I'll be at Rosses for another 20 minutes or so. You can reach me here."

He called his grandmother's house, but there was no answer.

"Damn," he muttered under his breath, setting the phone back in its cradle.

"You okay, Rand? You're lookin' a little frayed," Art asked.

"I'm all right. All right. All right, I think."

"Want a drink? On me."

"No thanks, not now, maybe, hopefully later. I would take another ice water though," he said.

What to do, what to do, what to do? He eyed his watch.

11:03.

The smoke from a freshly-lit cigarette drifted across the room. The old urge to indulge ravaged his senses.

Rand inhaled the scent, then shook it off. Self-discipline would suffice for now.

11:11.

He had told Venator he would meet him, but he had no intention to. He needed to think. To sort things out. There was too much going on, too fast. $200,000 was a great deal of money, but if his grandfather had left something for him in a safe deposit box worth that much he felt compelled to find out what it was first. Blood always outweighed money and the bond with his grandfather had been unbreakable.

Another ice water appeared in front of him.

"Thanks."

"Sure thing, chief."

He sipped it, peered around the room. Nothing seemed out of place, just the usual crowd in for late morning mimosas and bloody Mary's. He checked his watch. Seconds slipping by in a crawl. Waited, hoping Adam would call him. Damn. Damn. Damn. He stuffed his hand inside the backpack, felt the wooden box, was tempted to open it, but Rosses was not the place. Maybe he could walk to the library. It was only a few blocks away. He could find a quiet corner, maybe even a spare research room. He drained the last of the water. Grimaced. Looked at his watch again.

11:17.

No calls. The phone silent.

"Thanks, Art," he said, fishing a couple of rumpled dollars from his pocket. "Hey, if Adam calls, will you tell him I'm heading to the library and really need to talk to him."

"Sure thing, chief. Hope everything works out. Pop in later and I'll buy you a drink. You look like you need it."

CHAPTER ELEVEN

His head was clearing.
That was good.

The Advil finally beating the encroaching headache that had been hovering on his brain all morning.

Paranoia or not, he did not feel safe walking by the main road, so he ventured into the park, taking half-paths toward the city library. Since he moved to the area, he had grown to know the park intimately. He had walked its unkempt paths on frost-bitten winter mornings, stumbled over many a root during a late night walk home from the pub and even taken a young lady on a walk at dusk, where – barring the mosquitoes - they would inevitably end up by the creek, on a blanket.

Though afternoons in the park were usually populated by the cacophony of children or the colorful strides of eager joggers, today it was empty, the stifling noon heat pushing all inside to their air conditioned havens and Rand had the sea of thick shade from the outstretched arms of old growth and spindly pines all to himself.

"They will not be glad to see me at the library," he muttered, noting the lingering smell of Rosses Point Pub on his clothes.

He eased out of a thicket of uncut weeds onto a small plot of close-clipped grass and before him stood the library. Despite the virtual domination of the Internet, community desire and swelling city coffers had allowed the city to construct it. It was a gorgeous building, beset with tall, skinny windows, Frank Lloyd Wright-esque angles and all encased in metal and white stone. Rand re-tucked his shirt, took off his baseball cap and walked to the vacant front desk.

"Can I help you?" the voice came from behind and startled him. He turned to find an attractive young librarian. A veritable walking cliché, with thick framed glasses perched on a dainty nose, sienna hair pinned up exposing a nubile neck and a short sleeve fashionable sweater that only enhanced her swelling bosom.

"Yes, good day," Rand offered his most clipped accent, straightened his back and slid his library card across the cool, marble counter. "Could I obtain one of the private reading rooms for an hour? I have some research I need to tidy up before a presentation this evening."

The librarian gave him a quick once-over, stared a moment too long into his green eyes, and then reached for the key underneath the desk.

"Of course, just sign in. What type of presentation are you giving?" It was not a demanding question, but of true earnestness and it caught Rand off-guard.

"Oh...it is quite dull actually...A presentation on Modern Anglo-Irish literature with a focus on poetry," the lie spilled easily from his mouth as he recited his Independent Study he had finished several years earlier in college.

"Oh, how interesting. I just love Yeats."

"Oh yes, the best. Turning and turning in the widening gyre the falcon cannot hear the falconer."

"Ah, The Second Coming, such a great poem."

"Oh, yes."

Sensing the moment over, the librarian gave him the key along with a wistful look.

"Thank you, miss. I shall be back in an hour or less."

The librarian visibly blushed at the word 'miss'. Good lord, thought Rand, a bit of Yeats and a courtesy title, give me another five minutes, a bottle of wine and I could have her in the sack.

But pleasures of the flesh was the last thing on his mind as hc half rushed to the second floor where room A3 waited for him.

CHAPTER TWELVE

A small clasp kept the box shut, but it did not have a lock.

Rand opened it with ease.

Inside was a smaller box, loosely wrapped in burlap.

"What is this, a Russian babushka doll?" he asked himself.

But as he looked closer, he could tell this box was different. Much different. It was a glossy almost-white wood, like a bleached holly or poplar. Unfamiliar intricate symbols were carved on the surface. Hebrew or maybe Greek? Runes of some sort? Cyrillic? He had been too cocky in college to study the ancient

46

languages and now he chided himself. He definitely knew they were not anything close to English or Indo-European.

He ran his finger along the side. Very smooth. Only a barely perceptible slit hinted at an opening.

He slid his fingcrnail into it and lifted the top, then carefully eased each item out and placed them on the table.

There were three cotton envelopes, one distinctly bulkier than the others, all carrying a wax seal of the family's crest. The one on top had the distinct writing from his grandfather's fountain pen scrawled with the words, "Read this First!"

He picked it up, broke the wax seal and his eyes fell on crisp white paper. Black words born of a typewriter were hammered across its surface.

March 5

To my dear grandson Rand Patrick O'Neal,

If you are reading this, I have left this body on this earth and passed on to brighter lands. As you know, this battle with cancer has been tough, but mercifully quick. I have been remiss in writing this as I have drifted in and out of the daze of morphine the last few weeks. They have told me I could pass at any day now. I have unplugged the drip for a few hours to finish this as best as I can. Forgive the gaps, but there is so much ground to cover in the last 60 years.

I should have shared the information in this letter with you when I was alive, but I had sworn an oath I would never reveal anything about my work. I suppose it is only now in death, that I am free from this oath and that I can ask you for your help.

Please know, first that I love you, I respect you and I know you are up to this task. Otherwise, I would not trust you with it. I hope you do not resent this or resent me for giving you this burden, but there is knowledge that must stay hidden and things which must be destroyed.

The less you know, the less you will be in danger. I say this, because, I am asking you to take a few leaps of faith with this letter. (If you are reading this in my study, please help yourself to a bottle of my finest brandy kept hidden in the bottom corner of my locked desk drawer. If you cannot find the key, just break the lock. Obviously, I won't mind.)

In addition to this letter, there should be two more items in this box. One is an envelope that contains a map. It is a copy of an ancient map, but it is the only copy that exists. I hid it here years ago when I began to suspect a faction of an organization I belong to was planning to use it for the wrong purposes.

*They do not know I have it. At least I believe
I have been deft and smart enough for that. Now
I leave it to you. Not as an inheritance, but for
you to destroy. As I said, I could not bring myself
to do it. An oath is an oath, despite where it may
take you. This map is made of a material you have
never seen before. I tell you this because it cannot
be simply torn into bits or even burnt in a common
fire. Please, do not trust it to indolent garbage men
or a fireplace. It must be burnt and only the highest
temperatures can destroy it. Find an incinerator or
cremator – there are several in Atlanta – and have
it destroyed immediately. Make sure to watch it destroyed. Do not have it lumped in with other waste.
Then take the ashes and scatter them to the wind.*

*The other item in here is an envelope that con-
tains $4,000 in untraceable bills. That should be
ample funds for the incineration of the map and
any extra funds – I dislike using the word bribe - to
be paid for the special destruction required.*

*Again, I stress, no one needs to know of this,
especially your grandmother. When you receive this,
do this act suddenly and without telling anyone.
You probably have already read my will and my letters and you know how much you mean to me. But,
once again, I must thank you, especially for all your
visits the last few weeks.*

And finally, burn this letter. And do this all now. I cannot stress the immediacy of these tasks. As I said, I am fairly sure these items are unknown and you are quite safe. That is why I have placed them in this safe deposit box – even hidden to your grandmother. But, it is better to use caution, than to face unnecessary dangers. Completing this act should only take a day, but this money should cover any unforeseen expenses

I am fading now. I feel at last that my journey here is over. Silver lands ahead of me. This burden behind. Take care, my son. God's Speed upon your feet.

Remember,

Verum in Aeternum

Your loving grandfather,

Henry O'Neal

A light knock on the door startled him. He crept to the door, wishing he had some type of weapon with him besides his car keys now tucked between his fingers. He opened the door a sliver. The cute librarian waited with two older ladies behind her, peering in intently.

"I'm sorry, Mr. O'Neal, but this room is reserved for noon and it is five till. I hate to be a nuisance, but the Ladies' Genealogical Society put in the request a month ago and they are always early."

"The gynecological society?" he muttered.

"Pardon me, Mr. O'Neal?"

An old joke among Rand's college friends completely out of place now. He felt exposed. Embarrassed.

"Nothing, nothing, just talking to my notes."

Rand looked over her shoulder to see the wrinkled faces of two elderly ladies peering at him.

He glanced back to the librarian, a slight flush on her cheeks now as she stared at him.

"Ah…of course, of course. Sorry, time slipped away. Can you give me just a few minutes to gather my belongings?" he said, and then motioning with a hand, "Come on in ladies, I am just wrapping this up…Doing some old research you know, keeping the mind sharp on a lovely Saturday."

Sometimes he was so full of it, he loathed himself afterwards, but in this case, he would say whatever he had to pacify whomever he had to.

"Oh, we can wait," the smaller one said, nose slightly turned, a frown on her wrinkled face.

Rand ignored her, stood and very gently slid the papers back inside the envelope, into the box and the backpack. He slung it over his shoulder and gave the women a perfunctory nod.

"Good day, ladies."

He did not see anyone else on his way out, except for a few old men in the reading section who had newspapers draped across their laps on those ridiculous mini flag staffs. He edged out the door and back into the park onto the path to lead him back to his house. There was no time for the pub now, no time to make more phone calls, though he could stand a drink or 14. He needed to get home, get cleaned up and decide what to do. Raid the phone book and find an incinerator or a cremator open on Saturday? Or should he drive directly to his grandmother's house? His grandfather had never steered him wrong before, but this was out of Rand's comfort zone. He tried to slow his mind. A shower, a sandwich and a quiet walk and he could figure things out, he was sure. He could be back at the pub tonight with no worries.

CHAPTER THIRTEEN

He had cut through a hedge separating his backyard from the park and was walking toward his back door, when a voice shot through the quiet.

"You sure are keeping fancy company these days, Rand. Mercedes. BMWs. Real nice cars. Slick."

Rand caught his breath and turned to see Mrs. Brown, complete with her ever-present poodle, strolling around the side of his house.

"Mrs. Brown – uh, hello. You startled me. How are you?" he said, levelling his voice, keeping his anxiety at bay.

"I'm fine, except for this heat. This is a hot summer. Every summer it seems to get hotter, you know. I tell you, when I was growing up –"

"Mrs. Brown," Rand interrupted, "I hate to be rude, but I am in a hurry and need to go visit my grandmother," he said, knowing no one could ever turn down that excuse.

"Well, that is what I was coming over for."

"My grandmother?"

"No," she gave the conspiratorial smile, the slight tilt of the head she always used when passing on a piece of gossip. "There were some men in your house just a few minutes ago. Fancy company, like I said. Good lookin' men and well-dressed too. Much better than your usual crowd of those newspapermen you work with. I thought you were in trouble with them, maybe they were with the police. After they left, I came and knocked on your front door to check on you, but no one answered so I came around here and that's when I saw you sneaking around."

"Wait," he said, all of her words hitting him now. "Wait, you mean men were inside my house while I was gone? How many? When?"

She took her time, seemingly relishing being the oracle.

"Oh, three of them. Very well-dressed, like I said. Handsome, but serious looking. They were in your house for about 15 minutes or so. They just left a minute or two before you got here."

"Damn," he muttered.

"Pardon me?"

"Nothing. Sorry, Mrs. Brown. Listen, I've got to go. I really need to go."

His footsteps carried him toward the door. He could feel her stare on the back of his head, heard her words trail off.

"You in some kind of trouble, boy?"

CHAPTER FOURTEEN

I t was not a complete ransacking. Not the type you would see in your run-of-the-mill network crime drama, but they – whoever they were - had definitely been in his home and they had been looking for something. And Rand bet that something was inside the box.

"The letter, the map," he muttered.

They had done a great job concealing their entry. There were no busted locks or broken windows visible from the exterior, though Rand was met with couch cushions sliced open, pictures removed from the walls, books flung open and kitchen drawers slung to the floor, contents scattered.

"Damn," Rand said, this time his own voice scaring him.

He heard something thud in the bathroom.

He tiptoed to the front door, grabbed the baseball bat snug behind it. Adrenaline rushed through his veins and his palms felt slippery on the wood.

He inched to the bathroom door. Then panic overtook him, he rushed in, the bat held high and his voice quavering, "Come on, you cocksuckers!"

He only knocked down the shower curtain, the rod clattering on the floor.

Otherwise. Quiet. A breeze gently blew through the open window. No one.

"Shit. I got to get out of here."

Reason, reason, reason, he told himself. He was sweating profusely and his hands were trembling. Think, think, think. Get out of here? Go where? It doesn't matter. Just go.

He went into the bedroom, the bat still gripped in his hands. They had been a little more thorough here. He was greeted by drawers emptied on the floor from his dresser. His bed was also overturned and the mattress sliced open.

He looked in the closet. The briefcase was gone.

"Of course."

He reached to the back corner of the closet. When he had moved into the house, he discovered one floorboard slightly warped and he was able to pry it open with a slight push from a screwdriver. He had been disappointed to find it empty that day. However, he had straightened the board and fashioned the nook into a clever hiding place. Now he pried it open, scooped out his passport and slid it into his pocket. He also had his own savings of $500 squirrelled away in an envelope. He took the bills out and stuffed them under the insole of his shoes. His birth certificate, social security card and other sentimental items he left behind.

He set his backpack down and began packing it. Clean T-shirts and underwear. A pair of socks. Shorts. A pair of pants. A sweater. His cell phone charger.

In the mess of items scattered from his chest of drawers, he found some worn Rally world maps. He jammed them into the bag.

What else?

What else?

In the bathroom, he snatched up the necessities.

Where to next?

If he had been found so easily, his house searched so easily, there was a damn good chance they would be eyeing his car and have a tail set. His old Camry sat outside in the heat and he knew its beaten four cylinder wouldn't stand a chance against a new Mercedes. He also knew he was far from a professional driver who could outmaneuver or outdrive anyone.

He fought off the temptation to look out the blinds in his den, knew any movement in the front of the house could attract attention.

He took a deep breath.

Then he carefully crept out the back door and half-ran into the woods.

CHAPTER FIFTEEN

He began to slow when he reached the creek. It was a shallow rivulet that lay at the bottom of a wooded ravine on the border of the park. The unrelenting washed out noon sun and thick humidity were punishing and he was half-drenched in sweat and his breath ragged. He got to the edge of the creek and began to make his way across the water, half-dancing on tiny rocks when he heard noises behind him. A crackling and rippling through the underbrush, half-heard thuds of feet pounding.

Damn.

He turned.

Through the green foliage, maybe 50 feet away, he glimpsed the gray suit of Venator. Moving very fast.

Rand finished his wobbly run across the creek and charged up the hill on the other side. There was no trail here, just a serious slope never meant for hiking, a forgotten steep embankment on the side of a road. His legs straining, thighs burning, he pushed through the choked undergrowth, tiny trash trees and discarded cups and bottles underfoot.

He was manically grabbing at the roots of trees and pulling himself up foot by foot when the ground exploded by his right hand. What the hell was that? Another small eruption just above his head. What the hell? Was he being shot it? He had not heard a gunshot. Did they have damn silencers?

"Stop!" the voice at the bottom of the ravine yelled.

A thunk into a tree trunk just above him and Rand saw the gleaming visage of a long silver dart.

A dart? A tranquilizer gun?

He kept charging forward, churning the earth beneath his legs. He could just see the light breaking through the brush at the crest of the hill. Just a few more feet. He gripped another root and pulled himself up. A pain raced through his left wrist. He paused momentarily, then, using his legs propelled himself up through the brush, onto a sidewalk and tumbled halfway into the street where he was met with a blaring horn and a silver Honda Civic that just barely missed clipping him.

He stumbled back and met the ground, ass first.

He picked himself up and stood on the sidewalk, eyes scanning, frantically looking for a taxi.

Nothing but cars and minivans filled with the faces of happy suburbanites. Not even a work truck he could flag down for a handful of dollars.

He looked behind him through the steep thicket, saw heads and arms appearing through the brush, following the ragged path he had made. He was planning to run into traffic and make his way across the street, but the last sight he ever thought he would call 'salvation' appeared as an orange Mexican taxi coughed its way toward him.

Rand waved the car down. Got in the backseat.

"Where to amigo?" a cheerful voice with a matching grin turned to meet him.

"Anywhere, just go."

"Que? What? You in some type of trouble, my friend?"

"Just go, Damnit! Forward."

"I need a destination. You know. An address. I just can't go."

"Uh, Midtown. Midtown Atlanta, the MARTA station next to the High Museum."

The driver shrugged, "Okay amigo."

The car puttered off, Rand wishing he could will it faster. He glanced out the rear window and saw Venator sprint out of the underbrush. Their eyes met. Rand involuntarily winced.

"You okay amigo?"

The question again.

"Yeah, good."

Then the driver craning his neck into the rearview mirror.

"How about your arm? You fall or something."

Rand felt the warm blood now. He saw now it was not a dart, just a cut from the scramble up the hill.

"Oh, yeah, just fine. Got a cut hiking, you know. Tripped on a tree limb. It looks worse than it is."

The eyes of the taxi driver suspicious in the rearview mirror.

"You got a Band-Aid or anything?" Rand asked.

"Just a couple," the driver reached into the glove compartment. "But we can stop at a CVS, Kroger, anywhere you like, I -"

"No, that's fine. Just keep going. This'll work."

"Okay, amigo."

CHAPTER SIXTEEN

Rand leaned back in the cool confines of the taxi heading south on Interstate 75 toward Atlanta's hip Midtown District.

The air-conditioning brought him a temporary relief and he breathed in the air deeply, wiping his sweaty forehead with his shirt.

He had been too busy staunching his bleeding arm and making sure his backpack still held all his possessions that he barely registered the taxi was already gliding into a parking lot for MARTA, Atlanta's maligned public transportation system. There wasn't a baseball game underway or a music festival so the lot was half-empty for a Saturday afternoon, the blinding white sunshine lending a washed out look to the oil-stained pavement.

The taxi driver slowed down. Rand fished in his pocket for some money.

"You got change for a hundred?"

"A hundred? No, amigo. I'm not a high roller, like you."

"Here," Rand shoved the bill forward, "Just give me 20 in return and if anyone asks, I am going north to the North Springs station to meet some friends."

"Hey, amigo, who would ask, I – "

Rand shut the door, ignored buying a subway token, slipped over the turnstile and ran toward the stairs leading to the underground terminal.

As he reached the first step, he heard the screech of tires and turned to see the silver Mercedes screech to a halt in the parking lot.

"Damn it," he muttered.

He hoped they would question the taxi driver. He had no intentions of heading north to the North Springs station. He was heading south to the airport.

He raced to the bottom of the stairs hoping to catch a quickly-departing train, but his enthusiasm waned as the rush of warm air rose up around him signaling another fresh departure.

He quickly took stock of his surroundings.

Faux-Greek columns and wire trash baskets standing at attention. A quiet clatter of plastic bottles and whisper of paper bags drifting across the floor. No one else was there.

What to do? What to do?

A mechanical female voice interrupted his thoughts.

"Train 42 arriving in two minutes. Train 42 arriving in two minutes. Heading southbound. Stops include Civic Center, Mechanicsville and Airport."

The sound of footsteps clicking down the steps.

Fast. Nimble. Getting closer. Closer.

Rand wrenched one of the wire trash baskets from its spindly column and hid behind a column.

The footsteps reached the landing. Rand could barely hear the click clack of heels walking around. Cautiously. Deliberately. He hoped whoever it was would think he was on the train that just left. The steps seemed to stop. He could hear his heart beating in his ears.

"Train 42 arriving in one minute. Train 42 arriving one minute. Heading southbound. Stops include Civic Center, Mechanicsville and Airport."

Rand waited. Thought. He didn't know what type of chance he would have to board the train if his pursuer was still on the landing. It was a risk he could not take. He had to do something. Either go down fighting or go down running. He heard the steps again, barely audible, moving slowly, heels scraping on concrete. Definitely moving toward him. He crouched behind the column. Bent his knees.

"To hell with it," he thought.

He swung around the column, the wire basket over his head and ran straight ahead, a yell escaping from his throat.

He saw the back of a shaved head, began to turn and his eyes met Venator's. Empty-handed, a half-look of surprise on his face.

He reached inside his suit jacket and pulled out a gun, but Rand was too quick and bashed the wire trash can onto his head. The gun spilled from the man's grasp and slid across the landing. Venator staggered, but remained on his feet.

Rand didn't give him a chance to recover and lifted the trash can again slamming it down on the head. This time, Venator fell to the floor. A bloody welt on his head, but still aware, he tried to rise. Rand straddled him and delivered a solid right hook to his face. Then an uppercut from his left. He felt Venator's hand grip his sleeve, felt a knee in his torso. Rand swung again with his right, saw the man's jaw snap back. A trickle of blood on the lips. Rand had forgotten the brutal excitement of the act. The impact of fist into bone and tissue. The gratifying release of anger and, simultaneously, the self-repulsive act of watching someone reel back from his own body. He ignored the raging pain that spread across his fist and hit him again, this time feeling the soft tissue of a nose break.

The man's eyes were closed.

Knocked out.

Cold.

Rand kicked him in the stomach for good measure and was aiming another swift kick, when he heard the train whisper to a stop behind him.

He turned, half-guilty, hoping no eyes inside had seen him.

He looked around the platform again. No one. He saw the gun beckoning to him on the cool tiled floor. Walked toward it, hesitated, then kicked it toward the stairs. Looked around again, paranoia threatening to dominate his thoughts. Nothing, but the red blink of a CCTV camera in the corner

"Damn eyes everywhere," he muttered.

Rand hesitated then reached into Venator's tailored coat, fingers reaching for anything, only finding a wallet. He stuffed it into his pocket. A muted bell rang.

"Train leaving. Preparing to depart to Civic Center, Mechanicsville, Airport."

Rand half-ran, squeezed in between the pneumatic doors of the train as they closed behind him. Sat down on the sickly plastic seats, feeling conspicuous, just noticing the blood on his knuckles, the sweat glistening on his brow. Exhaled. His only other companions in the compartment were a punk rock couple ensconced in each other, tattoos and blazed hair lost in a blend of pierced kissing and groping.

Moments later, the only sound was the cool whistling as the train glided toward the airport.

CHAPTER SEVENTEEN

The plane was flying at a mild clip high above the Atlantic bearing east toward Europe. Purchasing a last-minute first class ticket on a direct flight to Shannon Airport in western Ireland had proved easier than expected. Rand wanted to wait until he could catch a plane direct to Dublin where some friends from his college days lived, but that flight did not leave for eight hours, while the Shannon flight was lifting off in a mere 50 minutes.

Damned if he was staying around in Atlanta another eight hours. Too much was happening, too fast. He was confused, but knew one thing: He needed to leave Atlanta.

A pocket of turbulence gave the plane a slight bump and Rand felt his muscles tense. He had not ridden in first class in many years and relished the plush seat, the extra leg room, yet his backpack stayed snugly pressed against his chest, both arms wrapped around it. He knew he needed rest. Was determined to grab some sleep. Needed a clear head, but the box and its contents inside his back-pack beckoned. He decided to revisit it later, did not want to risk opening the envelopes inside the confines of the airplane. There was Venator's wallet. He fished it from his pocket. Elegant calf-skin. Simple, bi-fold. Inside was a Georgia state li-cense that looked relatively new issued to a "John D. Squires, 101 Hammond Terrace, Atlanta, Ga." The picture on the card matched Venator's. Rand paused. Studied the card. Squires? Venator? Who was the man? He also found an American Express black card. No other cards or identification. But there was paper in the back. A few crisp $100 bills stood at attention among a few creased fives and ones. And behind the last bill was the busi-ness card for Mr. Mark Venator. Nothing special. Just like the one he had handed Rand a few hours earlier.

Rand flipped it over.

His heart skipped a beat.

The handwriting was extremely neat:

Rand O'Neal
2914 Reede Street
Smyrna, Ga. 30082

Thoughts ate at him, so many questions, so much change in so short of time. But what was he to do trapped 40,000 feet in the air soaring over the Atlantic? He looked at his watch. Three hours to landing. He tucked the bag under his arm and leaned his head against the seat. He resigned himself to the inevitable, let the gnawing questions linger for later, the hangover finally catching up, the adrenaline gently subsiding, the murmur of the 747 engines lulling him to sleep.

CHAPTER EIGHTEEN

"Coffee, sir? Coffee? Sir? We're landing in one hour."

Rand jerked awake, unsure, his legs akimbo, his knees aching. His neck slightly crimped from leaning to the side, his arm asleep from clenching the backpack which he still cradled.

"Coffee, sir?" the voice again. Rand focused on the face of a flight attendant, cheerfully leaning over him.

"Actually, miss, can you make that two coffees? Cream please. It will save you a trip later." He efforted a weak smile.

"Of course."

Rand's addiction to coffee had been a part of his life since he was 13. It did not give him the shakes or throw him into a fit if he did not have it. Simply, as he often said to his detractors which ranged from schoolteachers to ex-girlfriends, being awake made him a better person.

He grasped the porcelain mug in his hands.

Drank down both the coffees, feeling the warm liquid ease down his throat. Asked for two more. Then breakfast. A visit to the airplane bathroom. Tried to straighten out his mind. Formulate a plan.

CHAPTER NINETEEN

Shannon Airport had come a long way since Rand first landed in the late-80s. The Celtic Tiger had roared in the 1990s and the government had pumped enough money into its doors to bring the airport up to a world class operation.

Beyond the tarmac, Rand could just catch a few glimpses of the Irish countryside and its rich green gave him a fleeting, but solid, sense of place in his heart. He had been coming to Ireland for years. Ever since he was ten years old, his grandfather had toted him along almost every summer. At first, they had devoted their time to museums, studied the ancient Paleolithic and Neolithic monuments, the Viking remnants and other sites of historical importance on the island. But as Rand grew older, the trips changed tone and became more of a shared experience, than educational. They spent time hiking in Connemara, took a boat to the Aran Isles and cycled nine miles on the rocky roads of Inishmore. He also learned to drive in Ireland, navigating the narrow roads, barreling on the island's highways that darted into the forbidding northwest mountains of Donegal. He had even worshipped at Drumcliffe, the church where W.B. Yeats was buried and stood with his grandfather who uttered a simple prayer over the poet's grave calling him a brilliant, but misunderstood writer who once had it all and then lost it to dark gods.

All sentimentality was now lost in the heat of the crowd rushing toward Customs.

Rand scanned the faces. The guards. The clerks. The fellow passengers from other flights. Noted the innumerable CCTV cameras mounted at every angle. He saw nothing that appeared suspicious, but, then again, he didn't really know what he was looking for. The hour in Ireland was early - 5 a.m. – and the line through Customs moved briskly.

"Name." Words uttered from a rotund face, a bulbous nose with a bushel of nose hair, expressionless.

"Rand O'Neal."

"An O'Neal, eh?"

"Yes, sir."

"First time to Ireland, Mr. O – never mind," he said, as he opened the passport, "you've been quite a frequent visitor to our fair country."

"Yes, sir. I have distant family here."

"Very good. I have cousins in Chicago, so I like to visit them as well. We go back and forth across the pond don't we?"

"Yes sir."

"All right, Mr. O'Neal. Your visit. Business or pleasure?"

"Pleasure."

"Where will you be travelling while in our lovely country, Mr. O'Neal?"

"Ah, Cork, maybe Wexford and then Dublin," he lied.

The man turned and typed something into a computer, pleasantries dissipated. A minute passed. Two. Four. Five.

Rand felt beads of sweat under his shirt, a catch in his throat.

"Everything okay, sir?"

"Fine. Fine. Just these computers. Slow as always. Some reboot this morning from that Mr. Gates of yours and his Windows he keeps upgrading…always something, you know….ah, here we go."

The requisite stamp.

"Thank you, Mr. O'Neal. You're welcome to go. And welcome back. Enjoy your visit."

Rand took a few steps forward. Paused. Surveyed the situation. Let the throng of people surge past him. There was a set of bathrooms, a couple of water fountains and then beyond two exits that led from the terminal, a north and a south one. The south exit, however, was cordoned off for construction so the throng of visitors was slowly herded toward the exit on the north side. Rand scanned the crowd of people waiting, watched the occasional joyful reunion, hands waving greetings in the air, the rare white sign with a name printed on it. Anyone could be, well, anyone at this point, he reasoned. Everyone looked the same. Then he saw them. Two men. Shaved heads. Sunglasses. Standing rigidly, too damn rigidly to be waiting for someone at the arrival gate at this hour. A chill ran up Rand's neck. Instinct? Maybe. But why take chances? He was done taking chances. He delayed debating on his exit strategy for a moment and, instead, went straight to the bathroom, faking a grimace and holding his stomach.

The inside of the bathroom was close to empty. A man stood at the end of the row of sinks, using an electric razor. A teenager yawned as he sidled up to a urinal.

Rand ducked into a stall. Locked the door.

He figured he was being tracked. Somehow, someone knew he made the flight to Ireland. Knew what flight he actually was on. And as a reporter, he had pulled enough open record requests and listened to enough police scanners and SWAT briefings to know how to stay off the grid. He did not use his credit card at the airport in Atlanta. Paying for the ticket in cash. That was a small plus, but only a slight advantage because he knew he could also be tracked via passport. It was a long shot, but if these people had access to his daily whereabouts, it might not be out of the question.

Also, his cell phone battery had been dead for well over 24 hours until he charged it up to 20 percent during an extended stay in the airplane bathroom. He still had yet to turn it on, but as soon as it beeped into life, he knew he would be back on the grid. The thought of over paranoia crossed his mind again. But, who knew what type of power and information these people truly had? He remembered his grandfather's words from when he was a boy, "Take stock of the situation, use forced direction, then misdirection, think before you act, and when you act, act swiftly." Many phrases like that from his grandfather, a deft instinct and enough Sun Tzu reading had given him an advantage as a reporter. But as a man on the run? Time would tell.

Still, he had to make some movements, drop some bread crumbs to the right people, use misdirection for the others. He yanked the phone from his backpack, switched it on, scrolled till he found Shannon's free Wi-Fi service. First things first. He pulled the card from his stalker's wallet, typed in the name and address to 411.com

John D. Squires, 101 Hammond Terrace, Atlanta, Ga.
Nothing.

Tried again. Different names, spellings.
John Thompson Squires. Jon R. Squires. Squires and Squires, LLC.

No matches found.
Typed it into google maps. Address first.

A Harland Terrace. Terraces at the Highlands.
A Hammond Way.

No Hammond Terrace.
No match found.

Typed it as a business. Reverse searched it. Used a few more old reporter's trick and still no match. Though he expected as much, the revelation still shocked him. This was a well-faked driver's license. This person did not exist.

Damn.

Next, he sent a few emails, random, vapid words to work and friends about sports or good spots for lunch. Then he deleted everything on it. He also deleted his history. Next he googled maps of Cork, Dingle and the ferry times from Dublin to Holyhead, England. He let the browser stay on those sites for a minute or two, just enough time to make a full register in his search history. He also checked the bus routes to those cities. Then he exited the stall. Left the phone on. Put it back in his pocket. He threw a sweater over his shirt, donned the Braves cap.

The same man was at the counter running an electric razor over his stubbled cheek. Another man grunting in a stall. No sign of anyone else.

Rand approached the shaver.

"Trade you a brand new iPhone for that razor."

The man looked at him dumbfounded. Oh, fracking great, this guy doesn't speak English. Rand tried again.

"Trade you a brand new iPhone for that – "

"Yeah, fuck mate, I heard you the first time," heavy English accent, cockney. "Why the fuck do you want to hustle me a phone for this tired old razor?"

"Never mind." Rand turned.

"'old own. Let me see it."

Rand turned. Offered the gleaming new device to the stranger.

"A bloody new iPhone for this old razor? What's your game son?"

"Listen man, I don't have time for a game. You want it or not?"

"Now, wait a sec – "

"To hell with it."

Rand turned away again.

"Okay! Okay!"

They made the exchange, Rand dropping the razor into his bag, left the man holding the phone.

Then, not another word, and out the door.

CHAPTER TWENTY

He did not turn back to face the north exit where he had seen the men, but, walked toward the southern end of the airport. He slipped under one of the sloppily hung yellow construction ribbons and slinked forward, waiting at any minute to be reprimanded by airport security. Nothing. Something was on his side, finally. He kept walking rapidly, eventually coming into a vacant food court, the evidence of construction still scattered here and there: torn up flooring, electrical cords dangling from a piece of decimated ceiling tiles. Foot traffic was light with a few early morning construction workers who ignored him. A cheerful sign read: "Please excuse our progress." He stepped over plastic work tape, past the dark shops, eyes ahead and spied a line of taxis outside the doors. No waiting. He knocked on the window of the first available cab. The driver, who was half asleep, jerked awake and motioned him to get in. Rand nodded. Pointed at the front seat. The driver nodded. Unlocked the door.

"Thanks," Rand said. "I tend to get carsick riding in the backseat. How you getting along?"

"Fine, fine. Where to?"

"Uh, let's see. How about we head toward Ennis. Yeah, Ennis sounds great."

The driver, his gray eyebrows half-hid above the brim of a tweed cap, gave him a good look over. An American in his early 30s, grass and dirt stained pants, sweaty with only a backpack as his luggage. Rand could see him reading him.

"You know the fare to Ennis is about 60 Euros." A statement clearly, not a question.

"Yep. That's fine...actually damn. I forgot to change over my money – sorry I am just getting here in time for a funeral, my uncle just died and I hope to make it on time. Can I pay you – say $160 – that should work out to roughly 100 or so Euros, though I haven't checked the market this morning."

As he talked, he pulled a $100 bill from his wallet and handed it over forcing nonchalance.

The cab driver's eyes brightened.

"Sounds good. Off we go, then." The car, a relatively new Opal, lurched into gear and soon they were heading north toward Ennis. Rand was quiet. Thinking. Occasionally looking out the side view mirror to see if they were being pursued. Over a half hour and they were only accompanied by a few white-knuckled tourists trying their first drive on the wrong side of the road. Otherwise the traffic was sparse, but that could be expected at 6 a.m. in this part of Ireland. In Dublin, it would be the genesis of a gray rush hour, but here the risen sun gently kissed the verdant fields, patches of green sliced by the stone walls, the cerulean skies dotted with fast flying clouds, their plumes blown from the angry Atlantic.

"Where to in Ennis, lad?"

Rand saw they were entering what could be generously dubbed the outskirts of the Irish village.

"Ah, good question. I was thinking the train station - no wait, let's go to the bus station."

"Hmm...did you say train station?"

"What?" Rand asked.

"Let's talk," the driver said and he pulled the car off the road onto a shallow shoulder.

Good God, thought Rand. Not now. To his left he was virtually trapped, the car door only inches from the innumerable stone walls that line the Irish roads. The driver sat close on his right and the car suddenly seemed smaller than it was. He was weaponless, except for his fists and if this man had a gun he would have no chance to use them.

"Where you going lad?"

"What? Ennis. I said Ennis."

"Let's cut through the muck. You're on the run. I can almost smell it on you. Oh, don't get me wrong, you're not the shakiest I've delivered, but I see you checking that mirror more than most and if you really are heading to a funeral in western Ireland, even the worst of us wouldn't show up lookin' like shite. Plus you would probably know where the funeral was, not all talking about: 'Maybe the bus station, maybe the train station.'"

Rand was silent. Stared into the man's eyes. They were not threatening, just matter-of-fact. Rand was chiding himself. Too cocky. Too distracted. Not enough planning. Damn.

"I don't know who you are running from...but I know how to run and have helped a few good men, shall we say, run in the past. You have a good look about you. I doubt you are a crook or a rapist –"

"No sir, no sir – I am – "

The cabbie held up his hand and motioned for silence.

"I don't need to know. I don't want to know. But I can help. You can forget the buses and train stations. Whoever you are running from is probably watching them. They might also case the major highways, though that is doubtful. I see you were smart enough not to rent your own car. That is good. But, even if you think you are safe now, you're a fool. Eyes and ears are everywhere these days. Tell me where you are going and let me see what I can do."

"Thank you."

"Don't thank me yet, son. I've helped many a man on the run, but I don't do it for free."

Rand laughed. A refreshing laugh. What felt like his first laugh in ages.

"Damn Irish wit. Sell me a great pitch with a heart of gold and then come for the money."

The cabbie gave him a quizzical look.

"Hey, it takes one to know one as we say in the states. Now, let's work this out."

CHAPTER TWENTY-ONE

Two hours later, Rand was close to clean shaven – thanks to the electric razor from his friend at the airport - the whiskers of his beard left in a sink in a service station north of Gort. He also had a fresh shirt on and a cheap raincoat. His baseball cap was in a trash can and he wore a skull cap. Black. No logos. Innocuous.

All had come service of Michael Casey, the 50-ish cab driver. Casey had bought the clothes, bought the time for the bathroom at the Shell station in Ennis and bought them both an early lunch. This wasn't going to be cheap, Rand had reasoned, but having Casey go into stores and exchange roughly $1,000 of the currency had kept Rand off of any CCTV, seen anywhere in the streets or had any receipts of any type traced to him. In other words, he was still invisible, off the grid and slowly shifting his identity.

"All right, lad, we're approaching 300 euros now on the taxi fare. You still want to keep going?"

They had just passed the sign for exits to Galway.

"Yes, sir. Let's go a bit further north before I figure out what the hell to do."

Casey nodded quietly.

Rand knew he had more money, but had to figure out how to spend it. Where to go next? All he needed was a damn incinerator, but being Sunday in Ireland and with the Catholic Church still with a heavy hand, he knew most industrial businesses were closed.

"Casey, I've got a crazy question."

"There are no crazy questions."

"Okay, maybe, a different question. Do you happen to know anyone who owns an incinerator or who might have access to one?"

Casey spat out laughter.

"Christ on a bicycle, boyo. You are a strange case. No. An incinerator? What in the world would you need that for, I – "

"Never mind," Rand cut him off.

Quiet, except for the purr of the wheels on the road.

Rand had to get somewhere to think before planning his next move. He needed a haven. Even if just for a day. Where to go?

He sighed, then began talking out loud, trying to reason with himself.

"Galway is no good. Too busy there. Too old to blend in with the students. Connemara would be great. I love those mountains, but I can't hide out camping in a tent near Maam Cross for months while plotting a move. Westport is gorgeous, but, that is about it, no advantage there, either. Tiny town. Sligo is nice, it also – "

"- is pretty strategically located, too," Casey said. "Not to cut you off, but you've got the sea to the west, northern Ireland to your northeast, with tons of mountains in Donegal and eventually the Atlantic and beyond the north if Scotland or Iceland suits you. Of course, it all depends on what you're doing."

"Yeah, Sligo is good. Great location, near a good-sized city, but where am I going to stay?"

He knew the answer before it came.

"I can take care of that for you, too, if you'd like."

CHAPTER TWENTY-TWO

Three hours later, Rand was sprawled on a sunken couch in front of a piddling fire in a damp farmhouse outside of Drumcliffe Village, a small hamlet north of Sligo city that sat underneath the otherworldly visage of Ben Bulben Mountain.

Casey had delivered him as promised to a safe haven, or what Rand could consider one. The house was occupied by a fellow cab driver who only introduced himself as Sean. No last name attached to the man whose very being exuded a dark view on life to match his black hair and eyes. A banged up taxi sat crooked in the driveway, a tire missing, a rusted out piece of some machinery beside it. Rand could tell Sean wasn't initially appreciative of his unexpected guest, but after Casey took him by the arm and the duo talked outside for a while, Sean returned with a smile.

"All right then, Casey says you need a place for the night. One night."

"Yes."

"Fine, fine. It isn't the Taj Mahal, but I can get you something to eat and some tea or stout to fill you up. I have a shower, too. The best I can offer for a bed is a pallet on the floor."

"That will work."

"Of course, it will cost you."

"Of course. How much?"

"Um.." Sean rolled his eyes up in his head as if figuring the cost of a stay. "I'd say about 200 euros."

Damn. I could get a suite at a Marriot for less than half of that, Rand thought. But he knew the game.

"Sure, 200 euros and Casey will get about half of that for delivering the package?"

Sean blushed, looked awkwardly at Casey who just smiled.

"I told you he wasn't a dumb one. Look, he's already got us figured out. A smart lad."

"Yeah, I see," said Sean. "And does the smart lad have a name?"

"Just call me David. David Collins."

"David Collins?"

"Yeah, that's it. Unless you gentlemen could get me another I.D.?"

Casey whistled through his teeth.

"Every second, this one brings a surprise, I tell you Sean, he –"

Sean interrupted Casey's musings, irritated, "Can't do it right now. I need time. It's harder to do these anymore. You've got face recognition technology, bar codes, new names, addresses, everything... plus you'd have to take boats and try to sneak in through ports with a fake ID assuming I could even get you one...it takes time and money, I mean weeks of time, and - "

"It's fine," interrupted Rand, holding up a hand to the exasperated man. "Fine. Don't worry, just thought I would ask. I just appreciate you putting me up for a night. Give me 12 hours to get some rest and some food and you won't ever see me again."

The men nodded.

"I'm off, David," Casey said, again with a twinkling eye, a slight wink, then to Rand, "Call me if you need me. You can forgive me for not giving you my card for obvious reasons. But, you can find me. I'm with Shamrock Cabs. Hard to forget that name, eh? Just call. Ask for Casey, they'll round me up. God knows, they always do."

"Thanks," Rand started to rise, but Casey motioned him down.

"Don't move, lad. Get some rest. Take care."

Sean followed him out the door where he could hear the men talking in low voices.

Rand was slightly annoyed at the price and accommodations, but couldn't complain. These men were taking a risk. And they didn't even know how big a risk it was. At this point, Rand didn't even know what the exact risk was, except it lied in the box. He knew it was the map. Damn. What did his grandfather say? An inconvenience?

The door opened. Sean came back in. A plastic smile. Rand forked out 200 euros from his thinning wallet.

"Here you go and one more favor," Rand asked. "If you could fetch me a pack of smokes…and a small axe or a cricket bat, I would happily throw in another 50 euros."

A wry grin.

"A small axe? What are you a fuckin' dwarf? Been watching too many Lord of the Rings movies," Sean was enjoying this. "All right, never mind, be back in a few."

Rand heard Sean's boots crunching on the gravel outside his door. He cautiously moved to the window, peered out behind a rotting curtain and watched the man's form disappear down the road. Then he went outside and looked around. Ah. There it was. Peat. Piled haphazardly against the wall. He grabbed a few handfuls of the oblong bricks and went back inside. The fire was burning low. The embers emitting just enough heat to keep the house comfortable. Rand heaped the new blocks on top of the fire. He knew that peat didn't flare and burn like dry wood, but hoped he could conjure some type of flame. He had to burn the map. Be done with it. The letter too. His grandfather had written a typical fire could not destroy the map, but Rand could try. Maybe his grandfather's mind had been diluted beyond reason with the pain killers and cancer meds and he was delusional. Rand blew on the stack of peat, a few little flares shooting here and there, like tiny rockets, before disappearing again.

He gently pulled the box from his backpack. Opened it. Held the last unopened envelope in his hand. Carefully opened it. Inside was the map. Strange symbols greeted him across the top of the map, similar to the ones on the top of the box. Below them was a map, but he could not place where it might be – ink-like drawings of unknown mountains, hills and rivers. No towns. No legend. A compass. And more odd symbols. And the material itself was like his grandfather said, nothing he had seen, or felt, before. It was almost like a skin in his hands, but also had a synthetic feel. It was thick, but pliable. A polymer? Paper with a plastic matte or coating?

He lifted it to the light. Maybe a watermark? Nothing, not even vaguely transparent. Ran his fingers over the symbols again. They seemed slightly cut or burnt into the map. He found himself drawn to it, studying it, twisting it, eyeing it from different angles, trying to find some illumination.

Enough. The heck with it, he thought. He needed to be rid of it. He snatched a pair of tongs, grabbed the map and shoved it into the hottest coals, under the peat logs. He watched and waited. Nothing. No sparks. No sudden burst of flame. The map sat there, not even curling at the edges, not even the slightest singe on its surface. Rand let forth a sigh. Felt defeated. Trapped. Lost. He tried two more times, pushing it in farther, blowing on the fire, then quit. Nothing. He pulled it from the embers. Oddly enough it was warm. He let it cool then placed it back inside the box. Next, he extracted the letter from his grandfather and tossed it in the fire. It burnt easily, shooting silent plumes up the chimney. That was a start, Rand thought. He was farther along now than a day ago, at least. Feeling a small sense of accomplishment, he lay down on the pallet and stared at the dirty ceiling.

CHAPTER
TWENTY-THREE

He woke to the sound of a door jolted open. A thin wedge of moonlight sliced across the floor. A lurching figure stumbled in.

Rand carefully moved into a linebacker crouch, ready to spring and tackle the intruder.

A light switched on. Rand blinked and was facing the bleary eyed face of Sean.

"Good God son, you scared the shite out of me!" Sean said, a hand raised up defensively.

"Likewise."

"All right. Fuck. Here, I've got you a decent axe and pack of smokes –at their finest," he said, handing over a rusty axe with a split handle and a pack of John Players. "Sorry, I woke you. I stopped by the pub on the way home and had a swift pint -"

"Or two, or three, or four or five."

"Yeah, yeah, smart lad. You figured me out. All right, enough already. Good night."

"Good night."

The cold handle of the axe beneath his palm, Rand drifted back to sleep without dreams for the first time in years.

CHAPTER
TWENTY-FOUR

The smell of robust tea woke him. Checked his watch. 10 a.m. Not bad. He had slept almost 14 hours.

"Up now are you? How about some eggs and rashers?"

"Sure, sounds great."

Rand's back was sore from sleeping on the floor, but otherwise, his body was surprisingly spry. After a lukewarm shower and a greasy breakfast, his head slowly began to clear.

Where to next?

"Sean, you mind if I grab a cup of tea and take a walk? I just need a few minutes to clear my head, then I will be out of your hair and on my way."

"Sure," Sean said. "Fill up your cup, there is a nice little path behind the house that winds up a ways up a hill. You can actually get a grand view of Ben Bulben on a good day."

It was not a good day, though. An ashen fog hung over the hills, rogue rain clouds scudding in from the coast spitting bits of drizzle and mist onto the damp ground. June in Ireland, Rand thought. Some things never change. He zipped his jacket, slung his backpack over his shoulder and wound his way up the trail, finally getting a sense of where he was. He came to a small gathering of boulders, thick heather surrounding them, and sat down on the largest one, ignoring the damp. He was surprised to see that Sean's home was actually in a tiny valley, hemmed in by two steep hills. He could see the smoke sputtering from the chimney, an abused gravel road leading to its door.

To the south, just barely, visible between the clouds, loomed the crown of Ben Bulben. Behind him, the hill became higher. Between the mist and the steep path, Rand could not see the top. The smells again. A peat fire. The waft of dung. The occasional tang of salt in the air.

He withdrew the cigarettes from his pocket, eyed them suspiciously. He had not smoked in over four years, but his nerves were beyond frayed and he was surrendering to what he hoped would provide a quick respite. He cupped his hand, flicked the lighter, the flame coming to life, the cigarette lit despite the whipping of the wind. Inhaling deeply, he stared to the sky, pushed the blue smoke out of his lungs and tried to think.

Where to next?

He did not have a detailed map of Ireland with him, just a dated world map, but was sure he could ask Sean for the closest incinerator. There must be one in Sligo city, or at the very least in Donegal in the north. He could get another taxi if he needed to or even buy a bike and ride cross country. He had the money for it. He could have it all figured out and done in less than a day if he played his cards right and luck was on his side. And, so far, it had been.

He took another drag from the cigarette. Reached in his backpack he had set by his feet and extracted the box. The strange wood. Imagined he should destroy it as well. He pulled out the map. There was no trace of the fire from the night before. He studied it again, the symbols, mountains, forests, rivers, but it could be anywhere. Any time for that matter. Nothing geographical matched anything in his memory. Traced his thumb over it. He rubbed it between his fingers. Waited for something to click in his mind. Nothing. He put it back into the box, dropped it in the backpack.

"So damn strange," he muttered to himself.

He stared across the valley, the clouds still moving, could see the lazy lumber of sheep, white pinpricks against the patchwork green. He knew he was procrastinating, but it was worth it for just a moment of enjoying the bucolic landscape.

At first he did not notice the sound. It was distant white noise, like the gurgling of a creek or the passing of cars on a highway. But then he recognized it. The sound of wheels on gravel. Down below, he saw a black Land Rover pulling up in Sean's driveway.

"Oh, shit," he muttered, immediately stubbing the cigarette out and lying flat in the sodden grass.

He raised his head just enough to watch. Two men got out of the SUV. The one in the passenger's seat looked like a typical law enforcement type. No matter what country or what culture, they all looked the same. What the hell was it, some type of unsaid dress code, Rand wondered? Shaved head. Bulked up. Dressed in all black military fatigues. He did not carry a gun in his hands, though Rand could not see from the distance if he had one in a holster.

The second man was more distinct. Tall. Erect. Thin. He wore a grey suit. Blue shirt. No tie. Shoulder length silver hair. The bearing of an aristocrat perhaps.

They approached Sean's house together. A knock. Rand saw Sean come to the door. A conversation of some sort. Rand couldn't make out the words. Sean's voice raised, an indignant finger pointed at the men. A shout from the man in black, the man in the suit waving his arms to calm everyone down.

Sean appeared to be arguing again, his voice rising and falling. Then, a rainbow of Euro notes in the tall man's hand. Sean staring at the ground. A pause. Then he pointed. Pointed up the trail to where Rand was barely concealed behind the boulders. Sean reached for the cash.

The man in the suit pocketed the cash, reached in his suit jacket, pulled out a handgun and shot Sean four times. His companion went over and shot him a few more times. The two turned. Stared. Their eyes scanning. Rand trying to press his body further into the ungiving ground.

"Rand!" the tall one called out, his voice tinged by a distinct English accent. "Rand. We know you are there. Come down. We have business to discuss. We do not wish to harm you."

As he spoke, his companion began scaling the path. Rand watched. The man was quick, despite his massive appearance and was moving rapidly. Too rapidly. The gap was closing and Rand was sure he would be spotted at any moment. The man closed. 100 yards. 70 yards.

"Rand! Come on down, son," it was the tall man again. "I swear on your grandfather's name I won't hurt you. I swear on Verum in Aeternum."

The words hit Rand like the shock of cold water. His mind froze. The man had sworn on his family motto, Verum in Aeternum – Forever True. How did he know that? Why was he using it?

He was confused, but any chance of waltzing down the mountain for a conversation dissipated as he watched a pool of blood form around Sean's decimated head.

"Come on Rand! Time is wasting."

The man in black was getting closer, taking long strides as he scaled the hill. 50 yards. His eyes sweeping the heather like a machine. 40 yards. 30 yards. The shock of the moment wore off. Rand knew he was outnumbered and out-armed. Damn if he was going to wait. He slid backwards through the heather and then raising himself into a half-crouch began to run higher up the hill.

His legs strained and his lungs burned. A scattering of small rocks slid out from under his feet, he began to fall, but caught himself, hands outstretched, kept scrambling, waiting to hear a gunshot.

Then he heard it. The thud of feet on grass familiar, flashes of playing football, accelerating for a tackle, flared in his mind. He tried to pick up his pace, but the noise grew closer. Closer. Closer.

Then he was hit. Went tumbling, body twisting in the air, bouncing on the ground. He pulled himself up and began to run when he was yanked back, a strong grip on his right foot. He kicked instinctively, wildly with his left foot, but the grip did not loosen. He turned, saw the man in black fatigues, aimed a kick at the man's face. Struck it. A trickle of blood on his nose. The man winced, but did not loosen his grip. Rand half stood, aimed another kick at the man's face, but a vice like grip grabbed his ankle and turned it hard, sending him to the ground, pain shooting up through his ankle, his legs, into his hips. Then a swift clip to his jaw, leaving him dazed. Light sparks in the sky.

The man now stood above him.

"Get up, pup. Time to go." An American accent.

Rand expected to see a gun or knife aimed at him. But the man just stood there.

"I said, get up pup. Time to go. Don't make me hurt you anymore. I'm tired. Been chasing you for two days and I want to get some rest."

Rand started to rise, but the pain burned through his ankle again.

The man clearly saw the pain on his face.

"Did you a bad turn, did I?" a sadistic smile, then turning to a microphone embedded in his collar. "I've got him."

He nodded his head, looked at Rand.

"Well, you can't make it up by yourself, give me your arm."

Seeing no choice, Rand did as told, threw his arm around the shoulder. Dazed, Rand limped down the hill, aided by the man whom a second before he was trying to hurt.

"What the devil happened?" It was the grey suited man, again the clipped English accent.

"Just a tumble sir. You saw him. He tried to run, but I've got him now. Might need some TLC, but we're fine."

"Good, Eric, get him in quick. I didn't want him harmed and I don't want to be delayed."

The man in the grey suit approached Rand, eyeing him with a distinct glare.

"Well, well, Mr. Rand O'Neal." A shark like smile stretched across the tanned face that featured a silver goatee, full lips and dazzling blue eyes. "Ah, and I see you have your backpack with you. How convenient. Just what we need."

Rand didn't say a word as the man lightly lifted the backpack from his shoulders.

Compliant. Confused. Still dazed.

"We'll talk more later. We have a lot to catch up on. But now, we must leave this hovel. Come on, get him in the car, I have us a charter flight at Knock that's been waiting all day."

Rand was lowered in the backseat, waiting any moment for the sound of gunfire. The end of light. Death. Instead, nothing.

The two men got up front.

The doors locked automatically.

"Well, Eric what have you done this time? A sprain or a break?"

"Oh, just a sprain. A bit of ice and some rest should fix it in a few days. Just an old Ranger trick. It's all in the wrist, simple leverage and torque. More immobility, than damage. Something Venator should have used, instead of all the chasing around. Damn Brit, too arrogant to be direct."

The man in the grey suit spoke.

"And that is why we rarely use any of our overseas operatives, too damn jumpy. Too much brawn, not enough brains. They go native you might say. But forget Venator, Eric. How is our patient? Can you give him something for the pain?"

"The pain? Oh, of course, sir. Just a minute," then leaning back in the seat addressing Rand, who sat awkwardly, one leg strewn out on the seat, one on the floor. "Here we go."

He reached over and quickly jabbed Rand with a syringe.

"Don't move pup, this won't hurt a bit." The sadistic grin again. "Just a bit of morphine to take the pain off. An old World War II trick. Just a bit of help. I'll get you some ice once we reach the airport."

Rand felt the flood of medicine warming his leg, waning, then waxing, moving through his blood toward his arms, his neck. His head, slowly began to swim. He'd had surgeries before. A broken bone here and there, sustained during a football game, recalled the warm lull of morphine. This wasn't it. This was luring him deeper. Lower. Heavier. The SUV began to move. He looked out the window. The sheep still staring, half-nibbling on grass. The rain had passed. The sun had come out again and it beamed a buttery light onto Ben Bulben. The SUV lumbered over the hill. Then, Sean's body broken on the ground, the red pool around his temple now stilled. The door to the cottage open, smoke from the fire now drafting out.

His eyes were closing against his will. Numbness. In waves. Again. He began to nod off. Tried to lift his head. Numbness. Voices from somewhere else talking.

"You okay, Eric?"

"Yeah, just fine. A nick on the nose. Thankfully, it wasn't a straight kick, so it's not broken. He did give quite a fight though. Not quite the candy ass I thought he would be."

"I told you he was special. The O'Neals are any-thing but soft. Strange perhaps, smart, but not soft."

The gravel crunched softly under the car. The gentle lull. Then darkness…

CHAPTER TWENTY-FIVE

R and heard birds chirping, a faint rustling of leaves, felt soft cotton sheets under him. Gradually opened his eyes and was met with the sight of shadows and mustard tinted sunlight on a plastered wall. He felt heavy. At peace? No, foggy. Calm? No. Sedated. For a moment, he imagined he was in his grandparents' home in Atlanta. He could almost smell bacon frying, the scents of coffee and pipe tobacco intertwining in the air and hear his grandparent's voices drifting from the kitchen.

He blinked. Looked again at the wall. There was no plaster at their home in Atlanta. The faint smile on his face dissipated.

He rolled over in a vast bed and was met with a postcard view of two open Gothic windows, curtains billowing in the breeze. Through the windows, his eyes were met with blue-tinged snow-capped mountains, a thick, ridge line of firs running up the side of them. The light on the mountains was fading. The tired worn yellow light of a setting sun. A lone star hung in the sky.

Evening approached.

Still foggy. He felt like he had in college more than once when he had indulged too much during what he and his friends dubbed a 'forest party,' nothing short of a bacchanalian feast of music and wine in the wilderness. He could not remember how he got here, wherever here was. He blinked again. Tried to focus. To remember. He shook his head gently. The haze was thick, but not natural. No dry wine on this tongue. No acrid taste in his mouth. Thoughts, memories began to filter through the cloud. He rolled over in the bed, dropped his feet to the floor. When he began to walk to the window, a prick pierced his ankle.

"Damn," he said, lifting his ankle up for inspection. It was wrapped in a small ACE bandage. It wasn't that swollen or even terribly sore, but he could tell it had been tweaked. He lay back on the bed. Stared at the ceiling. And then a few memories, images began creeping back to the threshold of his consciousness.

The run from home. Venator in the subway. The landing at Shannon, the ride with Casey, Sean's hard floor, Ben Bulben's imperious visage through fog, a path from a perch behind a house. Sean again. Dead. The pool of blood around his head. Running up a hill. A tackle in the grass. The shot of morphine in the leg. The bouncing SUV. The pool of blood around Sean's head. Then it was all vague. He remembered glancing out the window of a small plane. "Heart rate," someone said. "Blood sample?" someone asked. Names in the dark. Riddles in the sky. Questions in between consciousness. Snippets of conversations. He knows all now. What shall we do? We'll be landing soon. Another shot. A Band-Aid. An IV bag. More medicine. Blackness.

He looked at his watch to see what time it was. What day it was. It was gone. Then he noticed. All his clothes were gone. He was clad in a white T-shirt and white boxer shorts. He looked around the room, his eyes scanning. Nothing but a blank desk, a chair and the bed. His shoes. Gone. His money. His I.D. The backpack. The box inside the backpack. The map.

All gone.

Damn.

There was a sense of panic. A sense of disappointment. Disappointed in himself. His failure. But above all, he felt anger. Anger at being subdued, chased, of being caught and, again, of his failure.

He exhaled. Again, tried to concentrate.

Assess his situation.

I must think this through, he thought. I must not react emotionally. I must use my mind.

He looked around the room again. This time, forcing observation to the forefront of his thoughts.

There were two doors. One was half-open and, as Rand expected, was the bathroom. He went in, slightly favoring his ankle, and was surprised by the stubbled face he saw in the mirror staring back at him. He had forgotten about that. He had done a half-baked job shaving his beard off with the electric razor and now the hair was growing back raggedly. He rinsed his face and drank deeply from the tap, the water cool and welcoming to his throat.

A knock at the door.

Rand froze. What should he do? How should he act? Where in the hell was he?

Another knock, this time slightly louder.

I must focus, he thought. I must stay calm.

He went to it. Opened it, just enough to peer out.

"Good evening, sir," a neutral voice from a plain looking woman, dressed in what appeared to be a traditional maid's outfit. Black dress. White smock. Hair in a bun. In her hands, she cradled a serving platter that held a large carafe of coffee accompanied by a small pitcher of cream and a cup. All were pewter, inlaid with onyx. "Good evening, sir," she said again.

"Ah, yes, good evening." Rand hesitated.

"May I come in and drop this off? Your clothing will be up shortly. Mr. St. James apologizes for the delay, but thought you might want some coffee and fresh clothes before dinner at half past six."

"Mr. St. James?"

"Yes, sir."

Rand nodded, trying to think.

"Sir," she said, offering the tray to Rand.

Rand took it.

"Uh, did you say dinner?"

She nodded.

"At half past six? What time is it now?"

"Six o'clock, sir."

"Thank you?"

"Yes, sir."

The door shut. Rand tried it. Locked from the outside.

The conversation had been so civil and matter-of-fact Rand had not noticed the absurdity of it. He had been drugged and stripped and had just had a conversation with some type of maid about dinner. Dinner? He did not even know what day it was or how long he had been asleep. But, he was also in dire need of coffee and drank in the steaming black goodness before a hot shower. An assortment of toiletries were laid out. He did his best to tidy his face with a razor, shaving underneath his neck to make a ragged semblance of a beard and was able to tame his hair thanks to a comb. When he emerged from the bathroom, a fresh set of clothes lay on his made bed. A pair of corduroys, argyle socks, a glen plaid button up shirt and a pair of black loafers. There was even a belt. Interesting, thought Rand. They don't consider me a suicide risk, just an escape risk. He dressed. Forced himself to think the situation through. Thinking and instinct had kept him alive. He needed to lean on his intellect and not let the unknown, the blatant fear of what was happening overcome him. He had to remain in control. He looked around the room, hoping to see a camera. He did not see one. There was a sole light overhead, the bed, the open windows. Of course, that meant nothing. Rand knew cameras could be installed anywhere virtually invisible.

The door knocked. The same lady greeted him and began walking, expecting Rand to follow. He did, noticed the wood-paneled walls, his feet clicking on marbled floor. At the end of the hall was an elevator. The elevator doors whisked open. The maid punched in the floor number 3.

"Mr. St. James awaits you. You will be dining with him in his private quarters, quite an honor indeed," she said smiling.

"Yes…yes…an honor," Rand stumbled with his words.

The maid half-prodded him into the elevator. The doors whisked shut and he watched the green numbers ascend to the third floor.

CHAPTER TWENTY-SIX

The elevator doors whispered shut behind him and he peered into semi-darkness. At the end of the room was a blazing fire which threw flickering shadows onto an arched ceiling. The only other light emanated from a few wall sconces, piercing the murk like tiny torches in the smothering darkness. Rand blinked a few times to adjust to the dimness. Used an old trick he had learned from traveling as a reporter on SWAT night raids. He closed his eyes for 20 seconds. Opened them. Closed them again. Opened. Closed again. Opened. Science debunked the practice, but a crusty Sheriff's sniper he interviewed swore by it and that was good enough.

He began to see outlines of things. He noticed the length of the room. Long. Rectangular. The floor was flagstone. The walls were ringed with floor-to-ceiling bookshelves stuffed with not only books, but sculptures, wood carvings, the occasional framed piece of art. Rand started walking forward. The fireplace was impressive. Almost six feet long and three feet high, Rand imagined it was yanked out of a Viking hall and could imagine a spit of lamb turning over the flames. A mammoth painting hung above the fireplace, a colossal landscape Rand took to be of the Bierstadt flavor, one of his grand landscapes of the American West.

There appeared to be two doorways to the room, both open. One on the left led into darkness. A light spilled from the door on the right from where the aroma of roasted meat, vegetables and fresh-baked bread wafted. Somewhere he heard the tinny sound of Mozart's 'Eine kleine Nachtmusik.'

Rand kept walking slowly forward. Waited for an announcement, a voice or someone to appear, anything to shatter the unnerving silence.

Nothing.

In front of the fire, four wingbacked chairs sat, accompanied by the requisite side tables, a few ottomans and even a couple upright ashtrays Rand had not seen since he was a child. He half-waited for a puff of smoke to emanate from one of the chairs.

It would be fitting for such a setting to have a classic villain staring at the fire, smoking and talking to him. Visions from his Gothic novel class in college whirled in his head.

The voice from behind jarred him.

"Ah, Rand, at last. I do apologize for keeping you waiting and for all of our, shall we say, unpleasant efforts to get you here," he felt a slight pat on his shoulder and a tall form emerged from some unseen entrance and stood beside him. A flicker of flame jumped in the fireplace and illuminated the face that belonged to the grey-suited man who had, along with the man named Eric, poached him from Sean's house. Sean, who is now dead, Rand recalled.

A hand was extended and, on reflex, Rand offered his own to find it in a cold, but firm handshake. The man gazed into Rand's eyes, not letting go of his fingers.

"Ah, Rand O'Neal, I never thought I would see you here," a long pause, the dancing blue eyes examining his face, remaining a second too long peering, then as if snapped out of a spell, "But, ah, I have forgotten my manners. Let me formally introduce myself. I am Kent St. James," the grip released, the man's hand falling to his chest.

A slight bow.

Stiff formality.

Rand was silent. More curious, than confused. He guessed the man in front of him to be in his mid-50s. Tall, thin, but healthy. Proper, but not off-putting. The hair swept back, shoulder length, but immaculately styled. And the eyes. Screaming blue of summer skies. Eyes that seemed to see right through him. But also something else. A hunger? An animalistic predatory look? A sense of something he couldn't place.

"Ah, of course, you probably recognize me from that unfortunate incident in Ireland – of which I am terribly sorry – but now you are on safe soil and away from any dangerous elements. Come let us eat. I've had my personal chef prepare us a lavish meal."

With Kent's hand on his back, Rand was ushered into the room on the right where a feast was sprawled on a stone table. A rack of lamb took center stage, surrounded by steamed scallops, French green beans with shallots, boiled potatoes, a loaf of bread, two bottles of wine already uncorked and a pitcher of ice water. All the food still had wisps of steam hovering about it and the bread, by the look of it, had just been pulled from the oven as two large pieces of butter sumptuously slid down its sides.

"You'll have to forgive my lack of service tonight, but we do have some rather delicate matters to discuss and - as much as I trust my servants - I would prefer for us to dine alone so we'll be stuck with serving ourselves."

Rand stood still. Hesitant. Unsure.

"Please Rand, sit. I understand your wariness, but, trust me, all I want us to do is dine."

What other choice did he have? The setting seemed innocuous enough, but, then again, he didn't even know where he was. Kent motioned. Seeing no other choice, Rand sat down in the chair with its back to the wall. An old habit.

Kent gave a slight wince and then a smile, revealing a line of flawless white teeth.

"Just like your grandfather," he said already cutting the lamb shank, "back against the wall, eyes always on the door."

"My grandfather?" Rand quickly recalled his family motto shouted at him from Sean's house while he crouched in the heather.

"Ah, we can talk about that more later, but yes, I knew him. A fine man. A *very* fine man. One of the best I've known, but such weighty topics are always discussed better on a full stomach and we've got a lovely feast set up this evening."

He sliced and served Rand a hefty chunk of lamb and the two helped themselves to the vegetables and wine – both bottles from Bordeaux.

The two ate in silence for minutes, Rand only able to contain his questions by indulging in the dinner, his appetite surprising him, overtaking his desire to remain cold, at length, focused.

Kent broke the awkward silence with small talk solely focused on the food.

"Damn amazing how our chefs keep finding this stuff," he said, eyeing a green bean on the end of his fork, "French harcourts and sweet onions in midsummer. And I do hope you like the wine. This bottle is a $300 Merlot from a boutique family vineyard. Good friends of ours. They do quite well, I think."

"Fine…Actually, excellent." Rand mechanically said.

All of the habits learned under the wing of his grandfather were embedded in him and, even in the midst of a surreal situation, he could feign courtesy and almost enjoy the subtle notes of oak and smoke in the glass.

"Very good. I hoped you would appreciate it."

An uneasy quietness, except for the scraping of forks and knives on porcelain. Then, "How is your ankle?"

Rand hesitated again. Then mechanically replied.

"Sore. Tender. But working fine."

"I imagine so, but it should be right as rain tomorrow. We had our doctors make it first priority when you arrived. Lots of ice and some other therapies. Amazing what modern medicine can do, isn't it?"

"Yes."

The forced mouthfuls and stilted conversation ended soon enough. After the last few morsels were cleared, Kent wasted no time.

"Very well, then. Charles can clean this up shortly. Let's adjourn back to the study and I can illuminate you."

The term, 'illuminate' struck Rand as quite condescending. But, then again, he was in the dark.

Kent closed the door behind them and led Rand to the main room where the wingback chairs waited. The consummate ideal for any men's club. Deep, plush leather, the raised grain slightly amplified by the fire light.

The two sat.

Kent didn't wait to begin.

"It's been a long, exciting ride for you the past several days. Here. Let's have a drink. Guinness is it?"

The look on Rand's face registered pure surprise for the first time all evening.

Kent gave a closed mouth chuckle.

"You do enjoy Guinness, yes? But also at times Boddington's, Tetley's, just about any porter, correct?"

Kent touched a button on his chair. Rand heard the sound of faint footsteps behind him.

"Yes, sir," an icy voice. Erudite. British accent.

"Ah, yes, Charles. The Guinness for Mr. O'Neal. And did you happen to pick up those Dunhills? He was thinking of having a smoke."

"Of course, sir."

"I don't smoke," Rand said.

Kent gave him a wan smile. Rand remained seated. Just when he thought he couldn't be shocked anymore, this man had ordered a drink for him and not just a drink, his drink of choice and he knew it ahead of time. Before he could ask anything, a translucent white hand appeared around the corner of the wingback chair, handed him a pack of Dunhills, one cigarette distinctly extended. Rand tugged the cigarette out and a lit match appeared in front of him. Rand puffed, sucked in.

"Thank you," he muttered, half-turning hoping to see a face, but catching nothing but darkness.

No answer. A slight shuffle, then a tray featuring a single pint glass filled with Guinness and a pack of matches was set on the table next to him.

He heard a deep sigh and turned to see Kent puffing on a cigar and holding a glass of brandy.

"Well, well, well Rand...Where should we begin? I suppose you have most of the questions?"

Rand inhaled deeply on his cigarette again, let the smoke take its time shooting from his lungs. Took a sip of Guinness. Another toke on the cigarette. Exhaled slowly again, buying time.

"Where am I?"

"You are at one of our facilities in the Austrian mountains, actually our European headquarters. The complex is built around, inside and underneath a restored Frankish castle first constructed in the 12th century. We, of course, have made modifications and improvements over the years, but it retains a fair resemblance on its exterior to its initial splendor."

"How long have I been here?"

"Oh, not too long. I guess three days or so counting travel. You were worn out, old boy, so we gave you some time to sleep and recover."

And you drugged me, Rand thought, the slight well of anger bubbling as he gradually woke up wearing off the last defenses of civility.

"Who is we? Who is 'our'? Frankly," and the temper finally rising, "What the devil am I doing here!"

Kent raised a hand.

"Settle down. Settle down. All in good time. Outside of your ankle, have you been harmed? Have you been ill-treated? Is your bedroom not to your liking? Was the food tonight not to your taste? Please, Rand, settle down. We are on your side."

"Again, who is we? And where the hell are my possessions? My backpack? The box from my grandfather? Just what the hell is going on?"

Again, the raised hand from Kent.

"Easy, Rand. Easy....Where do I begin?" Kent stared at the painting above the fireplace.

"Damn it, just begin."

Kent exhaled a thick plume of cigar smoke that sailed between them before being swept up into the chimney.

"How well did you know your grandfather, Rand?"

"Very well," or at least until a few days ago Rand thought, then pushed the thought back. "You probably know that. He practically raised me."

"But, there were some things you probably didn't know. Am I right? He, I imagine, kept some secrets?"

"Yes, well, maybe. I don't know. We all have secrets"

"Are we playing Philosophy 101?" a slight smirk, then serious, "Let me begin by saying, he was a good man. As I said earlier, a fine man. I knew him for almost 20 years and respected him immensely. One of the finest minds I've been around and a wonderful teacher and a mentor. But, what he left you was not his to leave, despite his best intentions. It is ours and whether he overlooked that or not, we need it to complete our work. The work we are doing here is of utter importance to our species. That is why we went through the great lengths to obtain the box, the map, to find you. And, for what it is worth, you did a very commendable job of hiding. We knew you left Atlanta for Shannon, but after that the trail went cold. We picked up your cell phone signal – excellent misdirection by the way – and we monitored the bus and train stations throughout Ireland and western England, but got nothing. Our drones were too weak to send up in that wild Atlantic wind so that gave us a major disadvantage. We still have no idea how you got to Drumcliffe and you could probably be well on your way to Donegal or further north by now if it wasn't for the mouth of that idiot you stayed with. He had a few too many pints, flashed too many euros for a cab driver in the sticks and ran his mouth at the pub."

Rand pictured Sean's body again. The pool of red around his head, his body splayed unnaturally on the ground.

"And now you are here. We had no intention of bringing you here, you need to understand. We had no intention of even meeting you at all. All of this could have been so easily avoided if you would have simply accepted the generous offer we made."

Rand remembered the $200,000. The suitcase. The face of Venator in his unruly house. The Georgia heat. His job. His damn curiosity. His curiosity that had propelled him into this world. That world now a lifetime ago.

"What about the map my grandfather left me? Where is it? What about my job? When can I go home?"

"Oh, we've taken care of your job. A phone call from one of the top doctors in Atlanta was made to your boss and you are out on indefinite leave. Well taken care of, I assure you. The map and the box, as I said, was never yours to begin with. What is next here? That all depends."

"Depends on what?"

"Depends on how you react to us."

Rand's fear dissipated into a quick flash of anger.

"Damn it, Kent. I am tired of this cat and mouse game. Who is us?"

CHAPTER
TWENTY-SEVEN

"Let me begin at the beginning, or as close as I can to it. No need to beat around the bush," Kent pushed the button again and another Guinness appeared on the tray beside Rand. Another Scotch in Kent's hand. Served neat.

Rand took a sip of his stout. Waited for Kent to begin.

"All was not lost when the Library at Alexandria was burned," he let it sink in for a minute. "And not mere fragments either. We're not talking about a few shreds of lost scrolls or signed parchments. More than half of it survived."

Rand was expecting something a bit more concrete. Something a bit more corporate or at least rel-
evant to the last hundred years. Maybe some gravity
or explanation given to what his grandfather had
written to him. Perhaps a simple code to explain the
unfamiliar makings on the map. But, this was completely unexpected. It must have registered on his
face. Kent looked amused, then raised his eyebrows,
beckoning a response. Rand did not disappoint.

"Pardon me?"

"All was not lost when the Library at Alexandria
was burned."

"You're talking about the Library at Alexandria?
What – 3rd century BC, Egypt, Library at Alexandria?
Greatest library in the ancient world. Is that what
we're talking about?"

"Yes. The Library at Alexandria." Kent's voice betrayed slight irritation at repeating himself.

"But it's been recorded as history. I mean, in every history book, class, oral history, texts, etc. that
everything was burned? Everything was lost. I mean
some scholars say it was Caeser who burnt it, others say it was an accident or malcontents, but it was
destroyed. Historians still bemoan the hole in history there, the decimation of public knowledge, the
shared stories of cultures, but…"

Kent's face remained impassive. The eyes looking dead at him. Waiting for a response. Rand took
the bait.

"No?" then, "Okay, let's say you're right. If every-thing wasn't lost, then why is it recorded as such?"

"Because if one has exclusive knowledge....one does not wish to share it," a look conveying a deep mischevity. "So one spreads the rumors, fans the flames – pun intended – and lets the world know it is all lost. Misdirection. Misinformation. I believe your grandfather taught you that. So, then, everyone be-lieves there is nothing left. All the information, the power is lost to the ages. Then, humanity has to start over, that's what they believe. Meanwhile, we kept the secrets of Alexandria, the ancient knowledge, the clandestine intelligence and, more importantly, we've kept it, for the most part, secret."

Rand could feel Kent's eyes appraising him for reaction and Rand made a conscious effort to keep himself composed. Concentrated on an impassive expression.

Kent raised his eyebrows.

"Questions so far?"

"Hundreds, but, go ahead."

For the moment, the curiosity in Rand eclipsed everything else and he sat on the edge of his chair. Reeled in by the words. Enchanted.

"So, with Alexandria we have kept the infor-mation concealed, hidden. And when we need it, we have used it for the Greater Good. To help our species. To aid in shaping our future. To giving us an advantage from, quite frankly, annihilating ourselves or reverting back to barbarians -"

"Okay, this is fascinating and all," Rand interrupted, "but it's not like Alexandria was the only source of knowledge in the ancient world. I mean, it was as close to an international library as you could get, but there were other areas of learning, of shared information. I mean, you can't act like that was the sole keeper of information and knowledge. It's preposterous. The assumption that – "

Again, the condescending wave.

"We know, Rand. Of course, there were many centers of learning in the ancient world, before Alexandria and afterwards. Cordoba for example, the work the Muslims were doing while Europe sat in its collective shit during the Middle Ages, the keeping of sacred scrolls in Ireland and Scotland after the fall of Rome, even great knowledge in the Far East allegedly kept under wraps to the West for centuries prior to the pyramids. Obviously, we are aware of that and have profited from it. But all that information tends to pale with what Alexandria itself held. And what was lost, or shall we say, found, when its contents supposedly burned."

Rand detested the smirk on Kent's face, but, again, his curiosity trumped his anger.

"What are you talking about?"

"This is a big sea to jump in. If you are really interested, we better start in the shallows. I don't know if you're up to it…"

Rand gave a silent nod. An acquiescence to the temptation.

"We have a few of the scrolls in this very room from the library. But, the real artifacts, the real treasure from Alexandria, the good stuff, as you might say, is several floors below us. Would you like to see them?"

"Yes, yes," Rand inwardly chided himself for his obvious enthusiasm, tried to push his eagerness back down. "But wait, original scrolls, which are – what 3,000 years old, give or take a hundred years? Here? In this place?"

"Oh yes, downstairs in The Cavern - that's what we call it, though it is more of a sacred cellar. Our elusive cache."

"Listen, this is all very interesting, but what does that have to do with me?"

"Rand. I implore you once more. Patience. All in good time. Let's start in the shallows. Now shall we descend?"

CHAPTER
TWENTY-EIGHT

They set their drinks down. Rand tilting his glass to drain every last bit of the stout. Thinking he might need every bit of nerve-calming fortitude.

He followed Kent to the elevator. The two walked in. Kent punched the button for floor -9.

The elevator descended. And kept going. And going. Rand watched the numbers.

-1

-2

-3

Rand could feel it growing warmer, could sense a slight pressure as the elevator plunged deeper into the earth.

"Good God, how far does this go? Are we really going nine stories below the surface?"

Kent smiled.

"Yes, we are going quite deep. Very deep. These are subterranean Paleolithic caverns that have remained in excellent shape. Over the last few centuries, we made many improvements, hollowed out more space, enhanced tunnels and added other creature comforts, you might say."

-7

-9

The elevator jostled to a stop.

The doors opened and Rand was met with the sight of two security guards, dressed in the consummate all black clothing. In their hands, they each cradled an M-16. Rand had seen the guns before, but these appeared to have been given the full gadget treatment: scope, mounted laser-sights and a few other modifications he couldn't place. A bandolier of grenades strapped to their chests. Two-way radios on their belts. Behind them, was a small desk where a computer sat and a bar code scanner adorned its white surface.

And, then, framing the entire scene behind the guards was an ominous door. At least ten feet tall. Dark stained oak, pockmarked and weathered.

"Security badge, sir." One of the guards requested mechanically.

"But, you know who I am, you don't need to see my badge."

"Sorry, sir. Orders."

Kent reached in his pocket and passed over his badge, half-confiding to Rand, "I hate wearing the damned thing pinned on my shirt like a computer repairman, so I just try to remember to carry it with me."

"Thank you, sir," the guard scanned it and handed it back.

"No, Johnson, thank you," and then turning back to Rand, "I always insist that he double checks everything, including the executive director's I.D."

"Guest, sir?" the guard said, tilting his head to Rand.

"Yes. Rand, kindly let them get a quick photograph and a temporary guest ID for you."

Rand did as told, stood for a quick photo as one guard transmitted his height and weight into the computer. A fresh card soon slid out of a printer located somewhere underneath the desk. Rand took it, felt the warm laminate in his hand. Before clipping it on his shirt, he saw his own odd face looking back at him through the plastic and then noticed it expired in seven days.

The two passed by the guards. Kent approached the door. Rand noticed a small panel beside it which he presumed to be a thumbprint scanner. Kent pressed his thumb firmly, there was a faint click and the door silently swung open.

"Ah, now for the fun," he remarked, self-satisfied. "This is what we – although it has a much more so-phisticated name - call The Cavern."

Rand followed him.

Again, half-darkness.

Rand squinted, involuntarily craning his neck forward.

"No need to hurt your eyes, son. You'll get the full tour soon enough." Kent beside him, standing impassively.

Rand remained silent. Concentrated on deep breaths. Closed his eyes. Opened them. The drill again. Stared down at a neat nicked parquet floor. Play it cool, he told himself. Reason. Not emotion.

"Well, shall we?" Kent motioned into the darkness. "Follow me."

Rand saw Kent reach into his blazer pocket and extract some type of remote control which he aimed at various points throughout the room. Wall-mounted sconces came to life, throwing long white rays upward. Rand followed their beams some 20 feet up where he caught glimpses of a rough-hewn rock ceiling, the color of cinnamon.

Around the room, he saw lines upon lines of bookcases stretching into what seemed like infinity. There were books of all types. Large books with uneven parchment which could have weighed over 100 pounds, small tiny books covered in a thin sheath of cow or ox skin, pages hastily bound with leather straps, and on four shelves alone, scrolls upon scrolls stacked neatly and placed inside clear fiberglass tubes, their ends numbered and bar coded.

Though the books came in all shapes and sizes, the shelves themselves were orderly in stature resembling the library at Trinity College in Dublin, though on second glance the endless rows looked like something plucked from an M.C. Escher painting or a journey within Alice In Wonderland. Scattered through the rows and mazes of bookcases were reading rooms, standalone desks, half-circles of wing backed chairs and a bevy of all types of antiquities behind hermitically sealed glass.

A museum. A library. A research center. The Cavern.

The area was noiseless, except for a faint hum that Rand suspected was a humidifier to maintain temperature.

"Impressive, isn't it?" Kent didn't expect an answer, but Rand was too spellbound to notice the pomposity and a breathless "yes" escaped from him.

He was overcome. So much knowledge. So...secluded. So...excluded.

"How much of this is secret, is, how do I put it, exclusive to you, not known to the public?"

A half-sneer took over Kent's face.

"Oh, I don't know," an overemphasized noncha-lance. "95 percent or so. Some are just rare volumes or different translations we keep here because it is safer than anywhere else. Your general Shakespeare or Beowulf ilk, but the rest, well, as far as I know, we are the only possessors."

This statement would have rendered most speech-less, but not Rand who had passed that point.

"Dear God, I could spend years in here," he tried to reel in the enthusiasm in his voice, to tap down his rising excitement, "How did you get it here? Is this all from Alexandria? How much have you read?"

"One question at a time, though I do appreciate your enthusiasm. We have a little bit of everything. A potpourri of Europe and some of its neighbors: The lost writings of Copernicus, a book of spells from 4th-century BC eastern Russia, stones from the depths of Atlantis that bear language few have seen, the real Arthurian legend culled from Druidic writ-ings ah, the list goes on and on…and like I said, most of it from Alexandria (the important bits), though we have bits and pieces we have salvaged from other places."

Rand's mind was spinning.

Kent's words broke the spell.

"Anything in particular you'd like to see?"

"Anything, in particular I'd like to see? Yes, every-thing!" He laughed aloud. "Wait, you said you really have Atlantis – or should I say Atlantean - literature, er, stones, markings?"

Kent smiled. "Most pick that their first time here." He motioned with a bony hand. "This way."

He led Rand to the rear of the chamber. As they walked, they passed more bookshelves, more sealed rooms containing ancient tablets, odd shaped stones and metals with strange markings. Soon, they arrived at what appeared to be a type of observation room. The glass was thick and the inside was dark. Rand had the feeling of being at a zoo, waiting to see what arctic animal was concealed behind the glass.

Kent pressed a button barely visible in the wood paneled wall.

A dim blue light rose.

Six tall standing stones, similar to the rings found throughout England and Scotland greeted them. They were not quite as thick or bulky as Stonehenge, but were tall. Seven feet high, maybe three feet wide. They were smooth. Perhaps marble? The blue light had risen to a white and he could see the stones clearly. Carved into them was a series of strange symbols that appeared to be a myriad of Egyptian hieroglyphics and Norse runes. Rand strained forward, his nose almost touching the glass, squinting to make out what the signs were, or meant.

"Oh, don't try too hard," Kent said softly laughing. "It took us two decades of working with the world's top philologists, archeologists and linguists to decipher it. But, then again, I think you might have seen some of those letters before."

Rand looked again, stared more intently. Then there it was. He recognized one, now two, now three of the symbols. The map. He had seen them before on the map. They were identical to the ones on the map his grandfather had asked him to destroy. The map that was now in the hands of Kent.

"Where did you find these? How did you find them?"

"Amazing, isn't it? The fabled lost land of Atlantis. Yet, here is a part of it. Most of it is gone forever. What is left in our culture is conjured in cheap movies and pulp fiction. The entire civilization was once a pinnacle of our species, then terrible things happened, followed by volcanoes, the sinking. The ruins sat at the bottom of the sea for hundreds of years, time eroding its already beaten crumbs. And then a mere year after we found it and began excavating, another earthquake on the seabed. Now all that is left is just crumbled blocks, indecipherable rubbage and it is buried so deep it will never be found. But we have these stones and hundreds of other smaller artifacts, jewelry, swords, shields and the like."

"I always thought it existed..."

"Of course, you did. There is something inside all of us that wants to believe. Mainly because it is true. Whether God or Devil. Good or Bad. Cultural consciousness. The steps between truth, legend and myth are only a few centuries. Child's play in the cosmos. But certain tales survive don't they? We want to believe, because somewhere we know it is true."

Rand stood amazed. Wanted more knowledge. Then, a pang of nagging guilt, as if he had been caught eating a piece of stolen fruit or sneaking a sip of his grandfather's wine when he was a teenager.

"But, why isn't this public? Why is all this kept away? Hidden?" a slight tinge of injustice through his wide-eyed wonder.

"The public can't handle it. That is why we handle it for them."

"But why? Why can't they handle it? If they are just antiquities or part of our collective history. Shouldn't they be shared? Part of the collective good or at least in the Smithsonian museums for people to see? Why do you keep them…here, under such security?"

"Because they all lead us to a greater power than you can believe."

"Like what?"

"Let's take a seat."

CHAPTER TWENTY-NINE

"Rand, there are places in the earth, literally in the earth, under the earth or beneath the seabed, that contain elements – stones to be exact– that can, shall we say, greatly increase our creative output, impart to us unseen knowledge and alter the very structure of our brain. They enhance our neural patterns, boost our synapses, dendrites, all of that good cerebral stuff. These stones give us the ability to think faster. To process more rapidly. To illuminate. To hyper create."

Rand was silent for a minute, stared at the floor, then back at Kent who awaited his questions with a bemused smile.

"You mean like a brain vitamin? Speed for the brain? Something like that?"

"No, no much more than say a vitamin B shot to the hippocampus or a dendrite refresher. We're talking light years beyond anything you've ever experienced or read about."

"And, wait, you said these stones. They are located in physical places? In the earth? Locations, latitude, longitude and all that?"

"Yes, didn't I say that?"

Kent did not expect an answer. The condescension in his voice was enough.

"Well, bloody hell boy. Don't give me a blank look. Again, and I do hate to beat a dead equine, this age is so daft to the world around them. Let's take a few examples. In all of your literary studies at your little liberal arts college, did you ever notice the proliferation of Irish writers in the early 20th century? Or perhaps, let's see, another example..." a slight frown as if thinking. "How about all the painters from the French countryside in the 19th century – Les Impressionnistes? The great writers from England's Lake District – Thomas Grey, Wordsworth and that reckless Coleridge? Earlier than that even – have you ever heard of a chap named Shakespeare? I mean really, do you think one man without help cultivated most of the stories, the themes, the very expressions of our language? Or more close to home for you – Muscle Shoals, Alabama. Alabama of all places, please," a slight snicker. "And yet there, a copious amount of music was produced. Do you think these are all co-incidence, ethnic realizations or some type of move-ments? No, these are all direct reactions of what we call The Slendoc Meridian. These events took place because they were either influenced or were above, or near, where parts of the Slendoc Meridian are."

"The what Meridian?"

"The Slendoc Meridian. Slendoc. The name is of old Atlantean origin so, of course, you don't rec-ognize it. It means quite simply, 'sacred' for lack of a better word though it has also been interpreted as 'magic' or 'light-giving' – 'illuminated.' It is not a straight line, like latitude and longitude, but was a curvature of stones that runs through the earth's core."

"A line of some supernatural like stone that runs through the earth?" this time Rand's tone was turn-ing purposefully sardonic, the incredulity of the last few days and the conversation itself catching up with him.

If he caught it in the diction, Kent ignored it.

"Exactly. We've only one major problem."

"And that is – "

"It's been broken up through the years. Plates under the planet's mantle move. Continents shift.

Earthquakes, volcanoes, you know the drill. Portions of the meridian were scattered. Other parts were destroyed all together by fire as what happened when Atlantis imploded. And, other parts of it, well, we really have no idea. Sunk below to the very earth's core? Self-destructed? Gone forever? Maybe. We still think much of it has not yet been discovered. But we're getting closer every day to finding more shards of it and over the last 70 years have come very close to completely harnessing its power when we do discover pieces. And the more we obtain, the greater the power gets and, as a result, our illumination as a whole."

Rand stared dumbly. This was all stuff out of a science fiction movie. Too much. His grandfather's letter? The odd map? Geological formations beneath the earth that act as creative energy sources? Atlantis? A clandestine group that guards secrets of the earth?

Kent cut off his thoughts, his stance growing more rigid, assuming the pose of a university lecturer.

"Actually, and though we have more proof on this issue than you could possibly fathom, it was known by our collective ancestors, but forgotten, or rather lost with the said burning of Alexandria. Other fragments of its existence lingering in either myth or history in other cultures we vanquished Any other oral traditions lingered for a few hundred years, but as humans usually do, it was chalked up to late night stories around the fire."

The self-satisfied smirk on Kent's face grew.

"Okay, wait a second..." Rand said. "Wait a second. Wait a second. Wait a second. You really want me to believe all of this?"

Kent raised his eyebrows at him, giving him a 'and why would you doubt it' look.

Rand stared at the floor, raised his head again.

"Okay, let's say you are right, just for argument's sake. If this Slendrac – "

"Slendoc."

"Okay, say the Slendoc Meridian does exist, why haven't we – er, geologists or scientists found it, yet?"

"Most geologists can't or won't detect it. They haven't either the machinery, interest or smarts. Frankly, if you do not know something exists, you cannot search for it can you? Our group, however, has a distinct upper hand. We know it exists and we've had a strong team finding it for centuries now. The best of the best. Minds that would make MIT and Harvard dons drool."

"So, what do you do? Do you just find these and extract them? Then what?"

"Our goal has always been to extract the fragments we find and then use them. If that is not possible – due to the depth or other geographical oddities - we purchase the locations above and around the pieces. Then we go to work where we use the stones as best as we can (they are quite dangerous to harness) to our and, ultimately, humanity's advantage. Of course, the largest shift in our history has occurred in the last few decades: Technology. Instead of ancient maps or riddles and pointless expeditions we now have machines and data and satellites and more innovations than you can imagine. While we cannot simply wave a magic technological wand per se, we can get a general idea and then use that technology to hasten our progress. We are now on the cusp of a new wave of discoveries, a new dawn."

"But, isn't there a bit of elitism that goes on, here? I mean, you are gaining a monopoly on these areas, while boxing others out. Who are you to determine who gets to create in these magic lands," it was with those two words, 'magic lands' that he realized again how foolish this whole conversation was, how dreamlike it came across.

"What, would you rather trust them to trash? Trust them to chance? Trust them to reckless abandon, so perhaps, a town drunk could have luminary thoughts on philosophy while he vomits on the very mantle of this sacred crust? Maybe you'd like to see some poor African tribe fail at writing a symphony? Maybe we could expose a pauper to it so he could grow wealthy and with his heart of gold help others.

Please, resources like these must be controlled, tempered and then wielded and capitalized on."

"Well, perhaps the drunk could become an artist" then reaching for words, "another master painter, a classical pianist. The African tribe could find a way to -"

"You don't think we're just using these for art do you? Please, how very noble of you. When I said creative output, I meant as in we create things, not some simple artistic pursuit. We use this power for advancing technology, medicine, genetic research, psychological exploration and, occasionally, military weaponry. How do you think the transformations in computer technology occurred the last two decades? Do you think your Silicon Valley icons started another technological revolution by hard work and staying up late at night burning the midnight oil? Some American dream nonsense born of the heartland and Protestant work ethic? Of course not. We recruited them. All of them. Brought them here for a few months, exposed them to some of our choice pieces of the Slendoc Meridian under the right conditions – oh, yes, all very secret of course. And, now look, nothing will ever be the same. They not only changed technology and the way people communicate, but ushered a completely new era, including changes in manufacturing, hubs of commerce, interconnection and more. Let the world idolize them. We don't care. We know who did it, or rather what did it and we can wield it any way we want. Call them all the children of Ozymandias if you wish. They will be forgotten soon and before the tides of sand erase their names, we'll have more like them. We are the wizards behind the curtain, Rand. The rest are mere puppets, players on a stage and all that rabble."

Rand silent. Again.

"A bit too much for one night, eh" Kent's face wolf-like, leering in the half light.

"But, wait. Wait. How can you – er we, us, whatever – be the only ones with knowledge of this? Even if you destroyed the other legends like you said, something somewhere had to survive. Tales around the fire and such. If there was evidence of this in Alexandria, there had to be writings elsewhere? It is almost like a Joseph Campbell myth isn't it? Archetypes, myths are everywhere, but I've never heard of anything near this."

Kent smiled again. A self-satisfaction.

"I told you, we have ways of keeping the knowledge…shall we say, sacred. Under wraps. Secret."

"Ways? I'm confused," Rand said, battling the urge to reach for another cigarette or throw his head in his hands.

"There are brutal angles, of course, but we try to avoid anything so animalistic so we work at disabling people intellectually. Hmmm, let's see, are you familiar with The Illuminati, The Knights Templar, all that drivel with the Holy Grail?"

"Yes, of course."

"All illusions."

"Illusions? Okay, I can buy into that."

"No, not whether you buy into it or not, but they are all illusions. They don't exist and never have."

"Wait – what do you mean?"

"Things, organizations, wild goose chases we created when people got too close to us. We made the Illuminati, then we set the seeds for its growth. We wove the mysteries about The Holy Grail. Invented the idea. Set it in motion. It is all a farce. I mean, please Rand, it's not even in the Bible. Seriously, the same with everything else these fools have been chasing the past several centuries. If they ever get close to the real truth, we create a new truth per se, stoke a new fire for them."

"But how? I – mean…I don't understand."

"No. Of course you don't. Not yet. Real power is not in conquering land or shaping politics – though we do have a hand in that as well - but in true change. Like the birth of the Industrial Age, the discovery of flight, the Atomic Bomb, this technological revolution we're undergoing right now. Our powers are far more reaching than you realize, Rand. What is the saying? A mystery wrapped in an enigma? Something like that…but that is enough for down here. This place itself can be overwhelming. Let us go upstairs. Have another drink."

Rand felt his feet guiding him toward the elevator. Again, the daze. The dreaminess of it all.

CHAPTER THIRTY

The elevator ride up to Kent's rooms had provided a slight respite from the shock of the revelations as Rand found some mental touchstones in the bland, familiar grey mirrors.

As the two of them rejoined their chairs around the fireplace, Rand took comfort in vice. While just a couple of days ago, he debated on buying his first pack of cigarettes in years, now he pulled one after another from the pack provided by Kent, virtually chain smoking as he unknowingly switched from sipping on his Guinness to quaffing. The firelight danced on the ceiling and Kent held court again pontificating, his glass of scotch a scepter, his wing-backed chair, a throne.

"We have been called many things, you know? By ourselves mainly, though occasionally by others. We were The Tutores for centuries. Latin for The Guardians or The Keepers. Then for a few hundred years, we called ourselves The Guardians, as our membership focused more into the Anglo-American realm. However, lately, we don't call ourselves much at all. We know what we do. That is all that matters. Who does it? Who, by name, cares? I prefer simply, The Organization. It is neat and efficient. Fancy names are nice, but we aren't here to show off, but to work. We prefer to remain invisible."

Rand sucked on the cigarette, drew in the hot smoke, cursed himself again as he did it, knowing this sin would not solve anything, but in an effort to keep any wits at all during this night, any prop would do.

He found his limbs loosening up. The alcohol finally sinking in. He was trying to measure his drinking, to indulge slower. He had to remain in control to some degree. To keep his composure. Knew the stout could loosen him up, unravel his resolution. He had to hold fast, like when he had been accosted by city councilmen at press conferences and had to keep asking the same question regardless of how angry the person became. He had to stay aware, like when he played linebacker and it was the fourth quarter of a game his body was tired and bone-beaten. But he knew he needed his eyes open to blitzes, to misdirection, to changes. It was all very difficult now, yet, fortunately for him, through years of discipline, almost second-nature.

"I still don't see how all of this," and Rand spread his arms wide, struggling not to slur "is a creation of you, The Guardians, The Tutores. The Keepers. However, you wish to translate it. I mean, the data, the historical texts that go into even legends like the Knights Templar is very detailed. There are scholars at respected universities that have made these very things their life's work. I mean dissertations, popular historical texts – hell, half of The History Channel. That just seems awfully hard to concoct."

"Rand, I keep trying to tell you. There is very little that is beyond us," a pause, "you look unconvinced."

"Can you blame me?"

Kent walked to a table in the corner and returned with a manila file folder.

"Maybe this will help. This was delivered to me just a few hours ago. Here is a very simple example of our recent work – work we've done in the last three or four days."

He tossed the file to Rand. Inside were three newspapers and a glossy sheet of paper. Rand pulled out the first newspaper, The Irish Times. At first he saw nothing unusual, then at the bottom of the page.

The headline: "Mystery solved in case of Drumcliffe drug dealer."

A photo ran beside the article. Rand looked closer. It was Sean. A happier Sean, taken a few years ago, by the look of it.

And then the story.

SLIGO – Two men were arrested late yesterday in the murder of Drumcliffe's Sean Behan, who was found dead outside of his home Tuesday morning.

Behan, who authorities had linked to a massive heroin smuggling operation out of Galway, was shot numerous times at his house. Behan's neighbor Michael Connell had heard the gunshots and rushed out of his home to see three brown cars leaving the scene driven by what he described in police reports as men, "of a tan complexion."

When Sligo Police arrived at the home of Behan they found him already deceased. Forensic evidence showed multiple gunshots from at least three different weapons which had been fired at Behan. Inside his home was found several semi-automatic machine guns, a large amount of cash and, on further investigation with the help of drug dogs, bags of heroin stashed inside a wall worth upwards of 100,000 euros.

Late yesterday evening, the special branch of Ireland's Intelligence Unit together with agents from Interpol apprehended two suspects in Galway, Juan Hernandez and Jesus Fellipes. The two men, whose passports registered them as Brazilian, confessed to the crime and are being held under high security for extradition.

"We haven't seen anything like this in these parts ever," Collins told the Sligo Post. "Even during The Troubles nothing like this. It's terrible."

Sligo Police have issued a public statement that this is an isolated incident and they have no cause to believe this is part of a larger operation on the western coast.

Behan, a longtime resident of Drumcliffe, is survived by his brother, John.

Rand looked up at Kent who gave a tight smile.

"But, he wasn't shot by three men, it was you and that other man and one car. Not, what, three cars? Brazilian? Large amounts of cash? Sean had no money, I –"

Kent held a finger to his own mouth.

"Oh, just keep reading. There's more in that file. And remember these are just the reports I received from our work in the field in the last week alone."

The next newspaper was the Atlanta Observer.

"Page B2," Kent said, annoyed.

Rand flipped quickly.

Headline:

Local reporter survives car crash, in stable condition

SMYRNA – Rand O'Neal, Atlanta Observer general assignment reporter, is in stable condition following a car crash that occurred late Sunday night near the intersection of South Cobb Drive and Concord Road in Smyrna.

According to reports, O'Neal had been driving southbound on South Cobb Drive, when he was struck by Bill Fleming of Atlanta who allegedly ran a red light.

O'Neal was taken by helicopter to Grady Hospital in Atlanta where his condition was initially listed as critical. However, doctors upgraded his condition to stable late Tuesday. Fleming was killed instantly. Toxicology reports showed a blood alcohol level of .08. Toxicology reports on O'Neal are pending. O'Neal has been working for the Atlanta Observer for three years and has received several awards from the Georgia Press Association for his work.

"Our thoughts and prayers are with Rand and we hope to see him back in the newsroom soon," said managing editor Becky Smith.

O'Neal is the grandson of the noted scholar and Atlanta philanthropist Henry O'Neal who died two weeks ago.

"What the fuck is this?"

"Oh, there's more. One more page ought to do it," a reptilian smile.

The Cork Courier
Page 1A
Freak accident kills Liverpool man

CORK– William "Bill" Gallagher of Liverpool was killed in a tragic construction accident Wednesday afternoon at the site of a new hotel, 'The Happy Shamrock' currently under construction in Cork. Gallagher had been electrocuted while inspecting wiring on the fifth floor of the resort. He had just arrived at Cork Monday afternoon after being appointed the new foreman of the project headed up by London-based Baston Industries. Gallagher had been working for the company since 1997 and had just been promoted to regional supervisor two weeks prior.

"He was rough and tough, but he always got the job done," said former co-worker Liam Boyd.

Foul play is not suspected in the incident.

"Who the hell is Billy Gallagher?" Rand asked O'Neal.

"There is a photo of him at the back of the file."

Rand dropped the papers down to the floor and lifted out a glossy print at the back of a file.

The face looked familiar, but it took him a second. Oh God, no.

The man from the airport bathroom he had traded the iPhone for a razor.

Kent injected into his thoughts.

"Yes, that was a tough one, but he was already involved whether he wanted to be or not. When we tracked your cell phone signal, we sent in four of our top security team members to apprehend you – a complete Black Ops set up – night goggles, laser sights on machine guns, all that good stuff. But, as you know, he wasn't you. After we stormed his – what we thought was your– motel room, we had no choice but to remove him from the equation… we didn't need any wild tales circulating from him about men dashing in his room in the night and that sort of thing. So he was terminated conveniently as an accident. It was after that debacle that I decided to personally come to Ireland and take charge of the situation."

Rand was in shock. His resolve, his control, finally decimated. His mouth dry. His ears buzzing, sight blurring. He barely heard Kent order two more drinks. Felt his hand grab the cool side of the pint glass. Drank deeply. Drank again. Tried to light a smoke, but his hand was trembling uncontrollably. Kent leaned over, extracted a silver zippo from his pocket and lit the cigarette for him.

Rand leaned back in the chair. Speechless.

"So, you see. This is just a mere three days worth of work on one case – that case being you. Think about it all in the long run, Rand. If we can do this with your journey to us, do you really think what I've told you about our other efforts the past few centuries so unbelievable?"

Rand knew it was a rhetorical question.

Shocked.

Drained the glass of stout. Found another waiting. Drained it too.

CHAPTER THIRTY-ONE

He awoke to the sound of birds chirping. The windows open, curtains pushed to the side, a faint perfume of lavender from some field. A scattering of clouds jetting over mountain peaks. Summer in Austria. Rand leaned over his bed, dropped his feet to the floor into a pair of thick slippers. He did not remember putting them there. He did not remember slippers at all. He shook his head, weaved to the bathroom to wash his face. He knew where he was, but was having difficulty piecing the night together. He remembered the first part all right. Kent's study. Dinner. Drinks. The descent into The Cavern. The revelations, The Organization, the Slendoc

Meridian, the shock of the newspaper clippings. But then there was more. More drinks. Blurred memories of shared stories. Even laughter? Kent's laugher? His own? Moving chairs. Swaying ceilings. The blazing fire. More drinks. Darkness.

He shook his head again. Kent must have dropped something in his drink. The blur on his head was not from anything natural, but medicinal. He felt betrayed. Naked. Unclean. Exposed. He half-cursed himself for not thinking of that at the time, but everything was happening too quickly and the time for judgment and clear thinking was short and narrow.

"Bastards," he muttered under his breath. "Using a damn thousand year old trick to get information. Bastards."

He was angry. Angry at the whole night, but more than anything, irritated at himself. His guard let down. He betrayed himself. He grabbed the tube of toothpaste and tried to wash the taste of sin from his mouth.

A knock at the door.

"Mr. O'Neal, your coffee. Brunch will be served in half an hour," a muffled voice announced.

Rand grabbed a robe laying at the foot of his bed, fastened it.

"Come in."

The door opened. It was the woman that had appeared last evening.

The same ritual as the night before unfolded. A carafe of coffee exchanged. A shower. Clothes laid out.

Now to eat again. And this time be careful, damn it, he told himself.

The knock again. The impassive servant. They would not be dining in Kent's private study, he was told, but rather in the Drachen dining room. The woman led him past the elevator to a flight of stairs that descended then opened up into a long hall. Iron-wrought chandeliers hung from buttressed ceilings, colossal oil paintings on the walls, oddly contrasting with the occasional video camera lurking in a corner or on a ceiling. The red eye always on. Then, the grand dining room. Elongated gothic windows lined the walls, heavy drapes pulled back so rays of late morning sunlight threw their buttery slabs across the table. The smell of coffee mingling with bacon, eggs and fresh bread.

Kent was seated at the head of a long table with two other men and a woman seated on his left. He stood, a smile affixed to his face.

The appearance of such a scene gave Rand the distinct feeling he was playing a role in a farce of a James Bond movie. The four villains, the fare set before them, he half expected some scientist wearing a Mao coat to come striding through the room holding a cat.

All humorous thoughts were abandoned at the now-familiar sound of Kent's voice.

"Good morning Rand. Please join us," he motioned to an empty seat.

Rand tentatively made his way to the table, cautiously eyeing the three other guests while they eyed him back.

"Most of our staff is tied up this morning, but I was able to pry a few away from their work to break bread with us. Let me introduce them. Doctor Virgillius, our head of psychological research and development."

He motioned to a man whose thin face was framed in a tightly trimmed black beard that matched his hair. Thick rimless glasses pushed back onto an oily face. Thin lips pursed. Bland white button up shirt. He gave Rand a slight nod and a stoic smile. No hand was offered.

"Sir Henry Cromwell, our director of commonwealth and international matters."

Cromwell stood and gave a slight bow. His entire body was the epitome of a British gentlemen. Short-clipped white hair and matching mustache. Erudite, stiff-backed and his very image bespoke of top schooling and decorum. And all this could be picked up despite the fact that he wore only a silk white shirt, grey trousers and a matching grey cardigan.

"A pleasure sir. I knew your late grandfather. A very impressive man. A very good man. He is greatly missed."

The words woke Rand up more than the pot of coffee he had drank earlier.

"Thank you, sir....I miss him as well....He is greatly missed, uh...A pleasure to meet you...too." Words stammered. Rand inwardly kicked himself at his fumbling.

"And our final guest, our requisite rose between thorns you might say, Doctor Hope Lightfoot, our director of cultural research. We were only able to tear her away after I convinced her that we had a budding writer and arts enthusiast with us."

"A pleasure to meet you," she said, the accent distinctly American.

She took Rand momentarily by surprise. After all the haughtiness from Kent, the cold formalities from the other two men, was a woman who looked completely out of place. Radiant green eyes, creamy milk skin, supple round breasts swelling from her sweater. All underneath thick raven hair, pinned by a utilitarian pencil, revealing an elegant neck. Rand could tell immediately, though she was beautiful, she either did not know it or did not care. He had met the type before. Too focused on a project to pay attention to their appearance. The project being either studying, volunteering or usually work itself. They were a rare breed. The beauty without the arrogance, the brains without the empty flirtation. Difficult to penetrate into their little cocoons of a world.

"Rand," Kent's voice, a sharp tone waking him from his musings.

"Terribly, terribly sorry. A bit of jet lag. It is a pleasure to meet you as well. I take it from your accent you're originally from the Midwest?"

"Well done," she said, a flash of a flush on her neck.

"He is quite perceptive," she said to Kent.

"Of course," Kent said, proud as a peacock, spreading his arms as if to display some invisible plumage. "I wouldn't want us to waste our time, now would I? But please, all sit. Enough with introductions, let us dine."

The food was pleasant. Actually, outstanding, Rand would later reflect. Omelets, fruit, croissants, broad slices of bacon and the constant refilling of French-pressed coffee. With the light streaming through the windows and the view opening to a well-kept stately garden, complete with statues of Greek and Roman gods, Rand could have fancied himself a Duke at a foreign estate, relishing breakfast before a day of hunting or writing.

It was the conversation and the company that soured the moment.

"Tell us," said Dr. Virgillius, "how have you found your stay here?"

The words were delivered with a faint Italian accent from a face that barely lifted its eyes from the plate of the food it was devouring.

Rand had been steeling his mind all morning to be firm and wary and passionless. Yet, he found something extremely distasteful about this man and wasted no time in drawing on his once-strong prowess of debates in English classes in college.

"That is a bit of an open question, but I would say, interesting. Perhaps even, exciting?"

A mirthless laugh from Virgillius. Then silence.

"You find that amusing?" Rand asked. He had always had little tolerance for passive-aggressiveness, a trait he distinctly learned from his grandfather.

"No, no. Not at all amusing. I apologize, I was thinking of something else."

And then.

"Well, would you like to share that with the class?"

The smart ass had arisen in Rand faster than he anticipated. But Virgillius did not rise to the bait. Instead, slightly inclined his head and studied Rand curiously, almost as if he was a specimen, eyes moving slowly over his eyes, his mouth, his chest. Rand was ready to fire over another vocal salvo when Kent cut off any further verbal sparring.

"Dr. Lightfoot has been working on a new treatise concerning Mozart you might find interesting," then turning to her, "Rand here is one of the few of his generation who actually still listens to classical music."

"Oh, really. How delightful." Rand almost thought she was earnest the words sounded so sweet. "Yes, Mozart and his symphonies. You know he was born here. Here being Austria. He did most of his early work in this part of Austria before being sequestered off to Vienna," all this said rhetorically. "But what most do not know is that he slipped back to the area quite frequently to compose. Yes, yes, he wrote some in Vienna, but his last good works were all written in the mountains around the Salzburg area where he would trek in the morning and spend a day or two burning through a box of quills and ink."

"Really? I don't remember that from Music Appreciation," Rand said.

A small chatter of laughter, like the ringing of bells around the table.

"No, of course not, you probably didn't see it in 'Amadeus' either."

This time Rand grew red.

"Oh, don't be offended. I do not mean to be rude. It was just one of Mozart's secrets shall we say. It was all recorded in a diary that we pilfered – such a rude phrase, but true – before the family could gather his belongings. History gives you the sanitized – as much as the poor fellow's alcoholism and gambling could be sanitized in later life – version. We found the truth. All this said, we are working now to find that mountain, or more specifically, that exact spot on a close by mountain where worked. We had a major breakthrough in the last 24 hours and I am planning to fly out there via helicopter this afternoon to assist our field team in what we hope is the final phase."

Rand nodded as if all this was part of a normal conversation, a regular day at the office for him, then found his feet.

"How are you, er, searching for it. I mean, I assume you have the diary as you mention so you are probably using that as a clue, but what other methods are you using?"

A wan smile on her face that was reflected on Kent's as well.

Kent took the lead.

"As Dr. Lightfoot said, we've had a significant breakthrough in placing the general area. Once we get a rough idea, we have several instruments we use. Our instruments are too sensitive and specific to use in a broad swath or anything like satellite, so we need a fairly defined location first. A primary mover so to speak," then cutting himself off, "ah, too much to get into over breakfast."

"And what is this breakthrough you both allude to?" Rand asked.

Kent shot Dr. Lightfoot a conspiratorial wink. Then looking at Rand unleashed the reptilian smile.

"We recently recovered one of our maps which I believe you know something about."

Rand's stomach knotted. He wanted to reach across the table and grab Kent, hurl his sinewy body to the floor, dash the plates upon his head. He feared that was the breakthrough. He knew they had it. They had stolen it from him. But the fact that it was being used. The fact that Kent was rubbing it in his face. The fact that he had failed all combined to fuel a rage inside of him. He restrained himself, took a deep breath, pushed the black anger down. Felt his head throbbing. Could hear his heartbeat pounding in his ears. His face growing hot. Another time, another place, he told himself. He still didn't exactly know why he was still alive besides an oath uttered by Kent in Ireland. Another time, another place, he told himself again.

He distracted himself with food. Focused on the moment. Grabbed another croissant, slathered a generous portion of butter on it and took a bite. The sound of his chewing seemed over-magnified in the stilted silence.

"Is this your first time to the continent?" Cromwell asked.

"Yes," and then thinking, but you probably already knew that. He decided to play along anyway. "As you probably know, I grew up visiting Ireland, Scotland and England every summer with my grandfather. And I studied in Ireland for a summer during college, but this is the first time to the mainland."

Cromwell nodded.

"Your grandfather was always very partial to the isles. All that creative Celtic blood kept drawing him back."

How the devil did this guy know his grandfather? What was their relationship? He tempered his spinning questions and directed a level line of questioning.

"How long did you know him?"

"Dear me," a look into the distance, a puttering of a napkin around the edges of the mouth. "20, maybe 25 years I guess. We didn't work together very closely, but a man like him stands out whether he likes it or not. He worked with me on some delicate inter-European matters with us pushing the Union together (mainly damned tariff and diplomacy nonsense). He was very skilled at maneuvering and understanding the importance of cultural history and psychological influences on that, you know. He was a brilliant humanist, but was also more of a scientist than he cared to admit. A deep thinker. A Renaissance man. But after the work was done, he was a load of joy. We would often stay up into the wee hours debating why American football was better than soccer and vice versa."

A look of merriment crossed his face.

"I enjoyed those times immensely."

A servant appeared and left another fresh carafe of coffee on the table.

CHAPTER THIRTY-TWO

Kent and Rand sat at the table together. Rand sipping coffee. Kent enjoying a cigar. Breakfast finished. The dishes cleared away.

Their three dining companions had left shortly after the meal, offering perfunctory farewells.

Rand could still not decipher if he was a captive, a visitor or a recruit of The Organization, so when he asked, "What's on the docket today?" he did not expect such a rapid reply from Kent.

"Oh, we've got you quite busy I'm afraid, thus the reason for the hearty breakfast."

"Oh?"

"Oh, yes. How would you like to accompany Dr. Lightfoot to her team's work in the mountains? We've got a helicopter taking off in half an hour. She took an earlier flight, but you could meet her and her team, spend the day observing their work, getting more acquainted with us. It should be quite interesting."

Rand was silent. Kent filled the void.

"Good, then. Your lunch has been packed and a pair of proper hiking boots and a rain jacket are in your room. You should probably get going soon."

Rand half-stood. Waited.

"Yes, Rand," Kent said as if reading his thoughts. "We used the map to find this piece of the Meridian. You know that. We had to. It is apparently quite a sizeable chunk. Don't feel bad about anything. This is ultimately what your grandfather wanted whether he knew it or not. We just feel so idiotic that it was so close, just miles from here and we did not even know it until yesterday."

Rand nodded. Silent. Eyes staring out the window. Playing a part in a play.

"Okay then, time to get going," Kent said, stood, clasping his hands with an artificial chuckle, "Enjoy the mountains. You can fly back with Dr. Lightfoot. You and I will do some chatting, then you can join us for our weekly formal dinner. These are fine affairs. Great talk, debate and intellectual discussion at these tables. Even I myself often keep quiet and just listen, absorbing the brilliance of our age. It gives me a distinct sense of order and hope to see such an advancement of our species together...Of course there is the food, too. Tonight, we've got wild boar, elk and Siberian tiger as the stars of the show, along with a hefty variety of vegetables, all grown locally and organically."

"Thank you," Rand muttered for no reason he could fathom, other than he did not want to stand there voiceless, like a child being ordered.

"Thank you," he said again, and then finding his feet. "I look forward to it, I also assume you have an amazing wine list."

That brightened Kent's eyes.

"My boy, you won't believe it."

CHAPTER
THIRTY-THREE

R and had only been in a helicopter once. He was writing an article for the newspaper and was invited to join three SWAT team members in a cramped helicopter as it wheeled incessantly over a meth house. That ride resulted in a case of vertigo, an upset stomach and partial deafness for a day from the sheer noise. It also resulted in him landing a Sunday front page story and later a first-place award for news coverage from the United Press Society.

This ride was much smoother, the pilot obviously more experienced and though they soared over evergreen forests and navigated through the blade-like summits of alpine mountains, there was little seasickness. This helicopter was larger, more powerful and less susceptible to a rough ride. It also did not hurt that Rand was planted in luxurious leather seats with plenty of leg room, instead of crammed into the back of a county-purchased machine inhaling spent gas fumes.

"You understand this is going to be a hot load-off." The pilot's voice burst through the static on the headphones.

"Yes sir."

"That means I am not going to land, just drop down low enough for you to jump. Takes too much gas and time to land, re-start and all that shit. Okay? Sorry, they've got me on a tight schedule today."

"That's fine," Rand replied. "Just let me know when."

"One minute."

The chopper banked, descended and hovered over a small alpine meadow, lowering its fat belly just feet off the ground. Rand jumped out and landed easily on his feet, the pain in his ankle completely absent. He ducked his head under the wash of blades and gave a quick thumbs up to the pilot who flew away.

Regaining his senses, he noticed Dr. Lightfoot waiting for him at the edge of the glade, hiking boots donned, a backpack on her shoulders and a slight smile on her face.

"Nice ride?" she asked.

"Sure."

"Good. Follow me."

The two set off into the woods and began to hike upwards. Rand taking his time, deliberately, slowly pushing one leg in front of the other, enjoying the rich scent of the evergreens, the soft spongy earth underneath his feet and above it all, branches gently swaying against a deep blue sky.

"Gorgeous."

"You think so?" Dr. Lightfoot asked.

"Of course, are you kidding me? Look at these firs. And the sky is so crystal clear this high up. Everything smells so fresh, so unspoiled, so vibrant… so clean."

She gave a little laugh.

"What? Does that sound too much like a Pinesol commercial, doctor?"

She laughed again.

"First, drop the doctor. My name is Hope, okay? And, no, it's not funny. The smell always reminds me of my childhood…We grew up in the country, outside a town in Indiana you never heard of. Our backyard opened up to woods filled with white spruce and pine. One spring, a tornado ripped through our county. Our house was okay, we were okay, but most of the trees in the woods were destroyed. Ripped from the ground, broken in half, their branches and trunks covered everything like broken matchsticks. It was a terrible site, a terrible day, but when I went outside after the storm passed, the smell of the crushed trees was so overpowering, so amazing. It was like a Christmas I only dreamed of or an escape into some otherworldly place. I wanted to capture it. That smell. Put it in a bottle…. open it when I needed it….I've never experienced anything like it since."

A few paces in front of him, he watched her head swivel back and forth gazing at the treetops, the sun splattering down streams in a haphazard fashion, finding its way in patches past the greedy limbs, a ray occasionally landing on the nape of her neck.

"I'm sorry," she broke the silence. "I imagine that sounds naïve to a journalist like you."

"No, not at all. I like it, it was poetic."

They hiked without words under the noiseless canopy of the trees. Then his turn.

"So is this what you expected?" he asked.

"What?"

She turned.

"This." Rand opened his arms. "Me."

"Close to it," she gave a half-smile, "But not as bad as the description from your file."

"A bad description? Me? Come on."

She lifted a raised eyebrow in playful surprise.

"Come on, what's in my file? More exactly, what isn't in there? You people are really obsessed with information. I mean, there's information and then there is an unhealthy obsession isn't there? J. Edgar Hoover obsession level. I imagine it painted me as a hell-raiser, a lost soul or something like that, huh?"

She didn't answer.

"I mean, I'm not a saint, but I'm not a bad person. I still enjoy a late night out, but I have never been accused of any serious crimes. I do have a work ethic, you know."

The half-smile again.

"I didn't say a thing, did I?" she said.

They continued their ascent for another quarter of an hour, the ground continually growing steeper, the moss and the dirt slowly yielding to rock, the trees becoming thinner. Rand stopped to catch his breath, leaned over, rested his hands on his knees, closed his eyes. Pinpricks of light danced under his eyelids and he felt a wave of nausea wash through him. He inhaled deeply, felt a tightness in his chest, tried to inhale again. Dizziness.

"You okay?" Hope asked.

"Yep," he gasped. "Just fine….Need to take a minute."

"Oh my gosh, I am so sorry, I totally forgot you haven't adjusted to the altitude. Did those bastards forget to give you something on the chopper? Please sit down. Here, take a break. You'll be okay in a minute."

She took his arm, helped him to the ground where he settled, his head in between his knees.

Hope sat beside him, gave him a bottle of water out of her backpack.

"Here, have a sip," she said. "This will help too."

Rand took the bottle, a taste of salt and ginger. Forced himself to swallow.

Then a prick in his neck. He flinched.

"What the hell was that!"

"Relax. Just some medicine to help you acclimate. It will accelerate the process."

"Damn. You people love needles."

"Please, Rand. You know it is quicker than a pill. Plus, what we use far outpaces anything like oxygen, a Gamow bag or Diamox. You'll be fine in a few minutes. I promise. The first time I hiked up this way, one of our team passed out because he swore he didn't need any medicine. Typical tough guy, stuff. You have a hard time beating Mother Nature up here."

Rand closed his eyes, began to lean back.

"No, you've got to stay in a sitting position," her hand on his back. "Just take it easy. Just a few minutes, I promise."

Rand leaned back over, head between his legs, his eyes still closed. Felt sunlight on his neck. Waited. Waited. Then slowly began to feel changes, his breathing regulating, felt his pulse rate stabilize, even a new energy in his lactic-acid drenched thighs. His shallow breathing began settling. Lungs swelled. Deep breaths now. Even.

"You're getting some color back to your face. Better?"

"Almost." Then thinking, why spoil a break? "Hope, tell me something. Is this all real, this Slendoc Meridian?"

"You still sound doubtful."

"Why wouldn't I? But, okay, let me ask you something then. Something more specific. Kent was full of grand examples last night. I guess he was trying to overwhelm me, to blow my mind - which he did - but can you give me something more concrete? And, I mean not just a period of time, or some group of mythic scholars or even Mozart, but something exact. Does that make sense?"

"You are the empiricist, aren't you?"

Rand didn't answer at first, then, "Well? Just give me another glimpse of what is behind the curtain? At least a writer or a painter, if not a scientist or inventor. I mean, just another name, no generalities, no historical phenomenon, just something I can relate to…this other stuff is too big, almost too easy to conjure."

"Okay, we can do that. I'll make it simple for you. Who is the greatest writer of all time?"

"Well, that is subjective. It depends on the period, their impact on the culture, their impact on the art form of writing, how many books they sold and what the critics and the public thought of them. I mean, these days one man's John Grisham is another man's John Steinbeck. That isn't really a fair question, I think if you – "

"Rand. Enough. Who is the greatest writer of all time? Who reached everything you just said. And not only reached those standards, but overreached them, in many ways, set the bar itself. Created a new lexicon of common sayings. Made the unique, the cliché. Created new standards. The most quoted. Dead for hundreds of years, but great. The greatest. You know. Some are born great, some achieve greatness and some have greatness thrust upon them."

"Good God. You don't mean Shakespeare. Shakespeare?"

"Of course, who else? No one, I mean, no one has come close, not only to his prolificness, but also the impact of his words. He saw into the human mind, didn't he? He was the archetype of the archetype, captured the essence of the struggle of everyone's struggles. He defined and refined everything, didn't he? How did he do it? How could anyone be that smart, that efficient, that brilliant?"

"But, that's still too general, isn't it? I mean, it is not even known if Shakespeare was one person or many. The man is a mystery. The first folio is a mystery unto itself. How much of his work was lost? How many lovers did he have? What did he really write? What did he borrow from Christopher Marlowe? Was he Christopher Marlowe? What about-"

"The lost years."

"Yes, oh shit…the lost years."

The medicine was working. Rand's focus was back now. His body, his mind sharpened, the nausea fading, yet still this revelation was unnerving. Hope answered his questions for him.

"Yes, the lost years. Two periods of the lost years, according to scholars. The first period was about fours when he was piddling about Wessex writing bad sonnets until he was seduced by Anne Hathaway. That was nothing really, a typical gap in history common to, well, commoners then when you were lucky to get baptismal records if anything else. But then, the real lost years. That's what you're wondering about. The seven year period from roughly 1585 to 1592. University professors would say he was honing his craft. He was developing a voice. A plausible explanation, of course, but really? Think about it Rand. You don't go from an amorous wandering school boy to the world's best playwright with simple practice do you? He had help."

"Help? You mean the meridian? The stone? But, what? You brought him here?"

"He didn't come here. I imagine Kent told you, this is just our European headquarters and – to be honest with you – we've only been here for about 100 years. No, Shakespearc's tutclage under the stone took place somewhere else, closer to home. We don't know exactly where. There is one school of thought that it was Northumbria. I believe he went to southern Ireland. Regardless, he was exposed to pieces of the Meridian. His mind was changed. Sharpened. Illuminated. According to the research I've seen, he was even given a sliver to take with him. A rare, rare treasure. But, for a rare, rare man. And he used it. You could even say wielded it. The proof is all there. Hundreds of sonnets, a ton of plays, the basis for our language today in many ways."

Rand stared at the ground, nudged aside a piece of gravel with his boot. Breathed again.

"Feeling better?"

She was standing above him, extended a hand.

He ignored it. Pushed himself up on one arm.

"Yep, better. Into the breach, one more time."

CHAPTER THIRTY-FOUR

A half an hour later, they came to another clearing where a makeshift technological center was assembled. A few generators hummed. Dozens of cords snaked underfoot linking computer terminals, a smattering of what appeared to be ham radios and obscenely large computer screens filled with all types of indecipherable data. Some of it flowing horizontally, other data running vertically. Numbers. Signs. Words. All of it fast. None of it making sense to Rand. Computer code? Algorithms? Oddly enough, on the opposite side of the computers sat an old fashioned corkboard on an easel with a map pinned on it. Several push pins adorned its surface which was also scratched with marks from colored pencils.

"Well, here we are," Hope said.

"All right, the million dollar question – where is this or what is this? Is this the location of the... stone?"

"Well, the stone is not here, but we are close and this clearing is the best place to set up all of our instruments and computers."

Rand noticed men and women scurrying about, clad in utilitarian olive shirts and pants. They all possessed a bee-like efficiency - checking clipboards and tablets, answering satellite phones, aiming some type of radio telescope to the skies, manically punching away at tablets or laptops.

"Quite a set up."

"Yes, you won't find anything quite like it anywhere else. It is a strange configuration of machinery, but combined it is used to detect a geo-magnetic anomaly in the earth's core. It runs throughout the planet in a – "

"Meridian of sorts," Rand interrupted. "Okay, Kent explained all that. Not to cut you off or be rude, but how do you find it? What are these machines? Magnet finding machines? You said geo-magnetic, right? Are these high-powered metal detectors."

"Not a bad analogy if you think about it. Very similar. However, instead of sending out a group of operatives armed with modified hand-held metal detectors – which could take months to comb over these mountains – we use a mix of satellite technology, digital map data, traditional map readings, underground radar readings and other options."

"Like what?"

Just then there was a commotion around the machines.

She turned her head.

Scientists clustered around the largest screen.

"It looks like they've found it. We've got it!" The voice came from a hefty man, whose thick Russian accent spat from a bushel of a thick beard. "Come see, doctor."

She ran over, Rand following behind, half nonchalantly. He took the moment to scan the woods around him. He could make a run for it now, he reasoned. All of the eyes were focused on the computer screens. He did not see anyone armed or any of the requisite black-garbed guards. He stopped his stride for a minute and thought about it. He could ease away and slink down the slopes with the canopy of trees making it harder to be spotted from a helicopter. He would hide in the day and run at night. He could double back up the slope then. That would work unless they had heat or infrared sensing technology, which they undoubtedly would. He imagined they also had dogs and more than the handful of guards he saw at the fortress. And, they probably were on good enough terms with the Austrian constables to dispatch a few dozen of them to participate in a manhunt.

Damn. Damn. Damn.

Another time, another place.

He finished walking to the work station.

There on a three dimensional digital map was a jagged piece of what appeared to be a type of ore glowing blue beneath the earth. From what he could decipher it was only a few miles away.

"That seems to be it," the Russian said. "That has to be it!" then a gibberish of excited Russian spewing out of his mouth, spittle landing on his beard.

"You're in luck," Hope said, turning to Rand. "Want to go for a ride with The Bear?"

"The Bear?"

She motioned to the Russian.

"Sure, why not?"

CHAPTER THIRTY-FIVE

The terrain was not terribly coarse, but The Bear's uneven handling of the ATV made it feel so. They bounced and barreled along the bones of a craggy ridge, slowly rising through the last of the tree line to the high slopes. The Bear and Hope sat up front, while Rand and a scientist with a forgettable face sat in the back, knees tight together, arms abutting.

"This is higher than I thought," Hope remarked. "To climb this high, he must have spent days up here. I imagine it would have taken nothing shorter than a caravan to haul up his items, but he was quite a diva in his day."

The Bear did not answer, only angrily eyed the terrain, a fierce determination in his eyes, hairy hands gripping the wheel.

Rand still found the concept of Mozart, white-wigged, dainty fingers, climbing up the side of a mountain to write music absurd.

"You really think he climbed all the way up here to write music? I mean, no piano, no soft pillows, no wine."

"Oh, yes, we do. For inspiration, artists will do about anything won't they?"

Rand considered all he knew. Thought about the past. U2 writing part of "Achtung Baby" in Berlin as the Wall came down. Bands like Pink Floyd and The Grateful Dead borderline destroying their brains on acid to climb over the barriers of consciousness. Jazz musicians like Charlie Parker and Miles Davis and John Coltrane pushing the boundaries of their very souls laden with heroin and cocaine in search of new sounds and then the long litany of rock stars who died, their deaths almost a cliché, a joke among the living.

The ATV continued to bounce along the side of the mountain, its red frame leaning dangerously off balance toward the valley below. Rand gripped the side of the vehicle.

Hope seemed to read his thoughts.

"Don't worry, we're almost there," she said, white teeth between the part of her lips. Gleaming. The mouth. Inviting. The rush of hair across her face gave her a flirty look. He could imagine her strewn on a bed, hair mussed and damp after a bout of love-making. Wondered about the body beneath those clothes. The curvature of her supple hips. Those breasts. The supple skin of her inner thighs. How could he think of sex at a time like this? Then again, with her around, how could he not? Her beauty found a chink in the armor he had been wearing since he arrived. He shrugged it off. Censored his thoughts.

The ATV veered back down toward the tree line where Rand spied four men waving. They too wore the olive jackets and pants. Three of them stood, holding what appeared to be a mashed up bastard-ization of long range radios and cell phones. One man in the center of them jumped up and down, yelling something in German or was it Austrian? His eyes were wide open, an etched smile on his face. He was manic, like the crack heads Rand had written about in the sordid alleys of Atlanta.

"Ich habe die Macht! Ich habe die Macht!"

The ATV pulled close and lurched to a stop.

"What's going on?" Hope asked, all of the levity of their conversation on the hike erased in a stern tone.

"We've found it doctor, I am sure," one of the sci-entists answered in heavily accented English.

"But what is this?" she pointed to the man jumping up and down, like a buoy bobbling in a raging sea, still wide-eyed, his hands waving.

"He says 'Ich habe die Macht' which means roughly, 'He has it' or, say, more like, 'I have the power' Madame Doctor," the man answered, looking very grave. "We told him not to go near it – the spot above it that is - but he would not listen. Now he will not listen at all."

"Weston," she said, then garbled out a stream of what Rand determined had to be German.

The man did not stop. He did not seem to even hear her.

She shouted his name again and repeated the string of German.

Nothing, but the repetitive mantra.

"Ich habe die Macht! Ich habe die Macht!"

"Damnit," she said. "We told everyone to be careful."

"I know Madame Doctor, we tried to tell him."

"It is not your fault. Sometimes it doesn't matter what we do, things just spiral out of our control. Just move your men back."

The men fell away, leaving only Weston by himself, springing up and down, his eyes alight, his voice sounded like a hoarse loop, "Ich habe die Macht!"

Hope reached into her backpack, coldly pulled out a Beretta handgun and shot him. The first two shots did not seem to register in the man's eyes. He stopped jumping, but kept repeating the phrase.

"Ich habe die Macht. Ich habe die Macht."

Confusion in his eyes, his body starting to slump. The voice slowing, dropping in octaves, but the words still sputtering out.

"Ich habe die Macht. Ich habe die Macht."

She fired four more shots. The bullet holes shredding the man's clothes. Forming an imperfect arc around his heart. He collapsed, his body still writhing, like a fish floundering on dry land, a snake whose head has been chopped off.

She fished a satellite phone out of her backpack.

"Send in a clean-up team right away. Make sure they are heavily suited up. We've found it and this area is hotter than we thought." A pause. "Yeah, we've got another one. Weston of all people…..he was a good one… Damn fools won't listen…yeah, he's still here" she looked at Rand. "I'll send him back with the chopper."

CHAPTER THIRTY-SIX

"Bit of unpleasantness you observed, eh? Sorry about that. Sometimes these things happen."

Rand was back in Kent's study, sitting in one of the chairs and listening to the voice he was starting to hate. He had been ushered in immediately when he landed and was handed a glass of Sherry and a cigarette, both of which he immediately took to, despite his reservations.

"Do you have any questions?"

Rand shook his head no. Gulped a dram of the amber liquid down his throat, felt the warmth spreading through his veins. Took a long drag on the cigarette. Kent motioned for him to follow him to a window concealed behind heavy drapes that he had not noticed the night before. Kent cast aside the curtains, cranked open a casement window. Three stories high gave them a prime view of the interior of the castle. Below, a tidy courtyard with flowering shrubs, exotic trees and bricks laid out in precise angles to form perfect squares. The late afternoon sun casting long shadows across the neat-nicked bricks.

Rand felt a tremor of fear standing so close to Kent in a faux repose. He blinked hard. Stared out the window, beyond the courtyard, over the rooftops to the mountains that looked ripped right out of a painting or a still frame from "The Sound of Music." A scattering of puffed white clouds tinged with edges of slate gray rode the wind over the serrated tips. Rand tried to enjoy the view, to find a semblance there, to find a peace inside of him, something to settle him…..but nothing.

"Again, sorry you had to see that. The power…the intense ferocity of the stones can be enough sometimes to drive one mad, unless you've learned to protect yourself against it or to harness it. To use it. To let it use you. Usually, we just discover fragments that are fairly unproblematic. Other times it is buried too deep to cause such a reaction as Weston's. Then we can isolate it. But sometimes it is compressed, it is mammoth, near the surface and the energy it emits is beyond anything we can control. And, as you saw today, the individual can't handle it. I am sure we all knew the one chap in college who couldn't handle his drink. Very smart, fairly clever, responsible, but give him a few pints and he goes mad. This is very similar. What you saw today has only happened a few times before in recent history and we warn our staff extensively. Obviously, some of our staff does not listen very well."

The words were delivered cold, matter-of-factly, a sense of scold on the edge of them. Kent's face revealing neither sadness nor pensiveness.

Rand nodded. It was not the first time he had experienced violence at such a close range. Working at the newspaper, he had witnessed the aftermath of many shootings and stabbings. He was not shocked at the violence. He was shaken, however, at how Weston failed to move even when confronted with a gun. The look in his eyes was maddening. He looked possessed. Drug-ridden. And he was jarred at how easily Hope had shot him. Remorseless. There was no hesitation, simply execution. Part of the job. Apparently, behind the green eyes and engaging mind was a calculating woman, whose desire to get what she wanted would not be hampered, by any means necessary.

"Another drink?" Kent was already lifting the sparkling crystal carafe, the Sherry's sweet currents carelessly swishing against the glass.

"Ah, no thanks, Sherry goes straight to my head," Rand lied. Truth was, he hated Sherry, but imagined it would be rude to tell Kent that. Knowing Kent, it probably cost thousands of dollars. This is ironic, thought Rand, this man might kill me soon and I am concerned about offending him. A wry smile crossed his face.

If Kent noticed, he did not comment.

Again, gliding on ghost stilts, the form of Charles appeared from behind them, the same bony hand extending a cold glass of stout to Rand. Wordless. A lifeless nod. Then he left.

Rand drank, followed Kent's gaze back to the courtyard below. A small cadre of gardeners had entered and were gently shaking a row of coifed beech trees. Dried carcasses of leaves dropped from their verdant branches. The workers then inspected the leaves before raking them up and depositing them into a trashcan.

They then inspected the branches and meticulously clipped any outliers with pruners, taking their time on every leaf, every branch.

"Amazing, isn't it?" Kent said.

Rand looked at Kent. Waited for the explanation.

"Yes, Rand, simply amazing how much we can tame nature, how we can shape it, use it, beautify it and, when necessary, bend it to our will. For example, this practice you just witnessed – the extreme detail to the hedge. They do this daily in the high gardens in the Far East. We learned this practice from the Japanese. Their horticulturists are the best in the world. Not only can they grow anything, they can tame it, too."

CHAPTER THIRTY-SEVEN

A gainst his better judgment, Rand had taken a nap after leaving Kent's study. The alcohol, the drowsy afternoon sunlight and the mere emotional drain of the morning caught up with him. The bed and fresh air provided a safe, though temporary, haven. He could've slept for hours, except for the nagging anxiety that brought him to wakefulness. He lay in the bed. Stared at the ceiling. Was startled by a knock on the door and the muffled voice of the nameless woman again.

"Dinner will be served in two hours, Mr. O'Neal." Drinks and hors d'oeuvres in one hour. When you are ready, I can escort you."

Why don't they use a damn speaker? Rand imagined they had the room bugged. Why all the old world formality? Granted, the castle dated back several hundreds of years, but with all the new technology, it was a strange façade, a needless gesture. The thoughts washed through his head as he took another shower, letting the hot water cascade over his body, hoping to rinse away some of the dirty day.

Again, while he had been in the shower, another outfit had been laid out for him on his bed. Pressed pants, tweed sport coat, a shirt and tie, wing-tipped shoes.

As soon as he had dressed, he heard his door unlock and slightly open. The woman was standing there.

"Follow me."

They walked down the stairs toward where they had eaten breakfast. Past the Drachen dining room, more paintings on the walls. Rand swore he saw a Picasso, a Van Gogh, a Gauguin. Soon, the cacophony of clichéd sounds of any cocktail party echoed through the corridor. The clink of glasses, laughter and confident voices sailing through the air.

"I think you can find your way from here, Mr. O'Neal," the woman said.

When he turned, she was gone.

Ahead was the entryway to the ballroom, two gothic wooden doors flung open. Rand took a deep breath, closed his eyes. Reason above emotion, he thought. Remain calm. Remain in control.

He had barely stepped in the room when he was assailed by Kent.

"Ah, you've arrived. Welcome," arms open as if welcoming the prodigal son home, except the waiting father clutched a glass of wine in one hand and an unlit cigar in the other. "Come in, come in," then looking over his shoulder, he motioned with a slight tilt of the head and a steward appeared with a glass for Rand.

"Fine vintage this is. 1873 cabernet. We've got a few hundred bottles in the basement we break out from time to time for special occasions. Our pursuit is noble, but these we lifted from The Third Reich's finest cellars during the liberation of Berlin," he gave Rand a conspiring wink. "And, with our finding today, tonight is a very, very special occasion. You, in fact, are witnessing a celebration of one of humanity's greatest discoveries during the last century."

Rand waited for him to expound, to continue the litany of The Organization's accomplishments. He was prepared to stand in stolid obedience while the man's hubris absorbed the area around them, but thankfully Kent was interrupted by a tug on his arm by a wizened older man, whose stoop and cane were at severe odds with the seething eyes of a canine hiding underneath tremendously large bushy eyebrows.

"Excuse me, Rand." The proper farewell. Then he was gone.

Rand was alone. He surveyed the room.

A hundred or so people filled the vast hall, a long banquet table dividing it in two. The familiar flagstones underfoot. The walls covered in tapestries. Lengthy banners and flags hung from its buttressed ceiling. The symbols on the cloths stretched across time and region. Flags of forgotten kingdoms, little-known sects and failed crusades. He thought he could decipher a few traces of the Welsh dragon, the thunderbirds of German legions, the odd dog heads of ancient Egypt. But many, he had never seen: Obscenely stitched dragon pendants. Blue birds ablaze on a gold background, their blood stained beaks dripping into a maroon sea. A single red triangle with a flaming torch above it.

Beneath them all, a crowd of a hundred or so attendees mingled. There were tall, elegant ladies, who looked plucked straight out of a scene of "Downton Abbey." There were a few gagglings of what appeared to be college dons huddled together. Tweed jackets, elbow patches, expensive school ties and ascots pinned to necks. And then there were the scientists. Even though they had shed their lab coats, they were still easy to pick out. Glasses. Intense eyes. Their dress was plain, utilitarian. Pressed dress shirts, wool pants and the occasional blue blazer.

Even for an event such as this, they came for work, not for pleasure.

"Hello, there."

The soft voice came behind him, interrupting his half-dazed observations.

He turned to see Hope.

"Hello," he answered, a stiffness in his voice.

"Feeling better?" she asked.

"Feeling better? I feel fine. Probably a little too much to drink before dinner, if such a thing is possible," a trace of his wit rising to the surface.

"I meant…after this afternoon…after that terribly unfortunate business with Weston."

"Oh, that. No, I am fine. That was nothing. Kent explained. I understand. One must preserve...these things." He was getting quite good at lying now. It almost began to disturb him, living a double life, having two faces, one to show, one to hide. But his means for survival trumped any guilt, though he had never heard murder described as clinically as "terrible business" before.

"Yes, they must be preserved." Her face darkened. "I do not like those things, those measures we, er, I, had to take today. That is not really me. But I had to do it. Had he lived he would have suffered terrible permanent damage. What I did is something I learned from The Organization, that the greater good is bigger than any of us individually."

"Quoting Star Trek now or Billy Bud?" Rand wisecracked.

A vague smile on her face. Honest eyes gazed back at him. Rand thought he detected a slight welling of tears in them.

"I am sorry you had to see that...I don't know what else to say."

She turned to walk away.

"Hey," Rand grabbed her arm. "Don't leave me here alone. I don't know these people. Keep me company for a minute or two."

She gave a stiff smile.

"Have you tried this vintage yet," Rand offered, taking a deep gulp.

"Oh, yes. Great year."

"It is damn good...Kent sure loves his wine."

"I don't know if Kent knows the word 'love.' But if he does love anything other than himself, wine would be near the top of the list."

Their conversation was interrupted by the man himself who now stood near the end of the hall at the head of the table, dinging a tiny coffee spoon against his glass, its ringing barely above the crowd.

"Quiet please, quiet please. I know we are all very excited after this unprecedented day –"

A roar of clapping filled the hall. Kent didn't seem to mind in the least, but simply gave a short bow and a smile. His eyes radiating with a self-gratified greed. He lifted his arms out to quiet the crowd.

"Enough, enough. We will all review this later and then be debriefed in a more appropriate setting at another time. But before we begin our dinner, our celebration, I did want to point out a few distinguished guests we have with us tonight at this most momentous occasion."

Rand felt a thousand eyes scan the room.

"First, we have Dr. Anne Catherick. Dr. Catherick is here from Stanford for a few days for an interview. We are hoping," and he leaned on the word, "hoping, she will accept a tenured position here before Thursday when her plane leaves. Her background is psychiatry, but she is also, shall we say, cross-trained, in neo-psychological inference and other new mind-focusing techniques."

Dr. Catherick, a lithe woman with close cropped blond hair emerged from the crowd and offered a quick half-wave.

A smattering of polite hand claps.

"We also have the brief, though happy, return of Conor Renfield. Conor, as most of you all know, is not a guest per se, but he has been busy working with our South Pacific headquarters for the past year. It is with great fortune, he arrived late last night just in time for today's news. Welcome home, son."

A tall, handsome man emerged from the crowd. Half stubble on his deeply tanned face. He took a self-deprecating bow, with a flourish of the hands. Polite laughter followed.

"And we are joined by a rather atypical guest, Rand O'Neal. Many of you worked with his grandfather Henry O'Neal, who helped head our international affairs division and, later, played a major role in our EU work. Henry died a few weeks ago and through some surprising circumstances, Rand has found his way to our circle this evening."

All eyes on me, thought Rand. He achieved a close-lipped smile, gave a slight bow, raised his glass to Kent. There was an uncomfortable hush, then someone started to clap. More joined in, the applause spread and grew. One voice from the back of the room cried out, "Here, here to Henry. He would be a proud man today."

Rand greeted many eyes with his own, mimicked polite nods, mouthed 'thank you.'

Glasses were raised. Emptied.

"Now," Kent announced, "let us dine!"

Clapping again. Rand followed Hope to the table, eager to steal a seat by her side.

Dinner bordered on the obscene, a feast that even Dante might find overboard with its gluttony.

Six courses were served. Rare beast and fowl, artfully piled vegetables with demi glaze sauce, confit, and foie gras. And despite how much or how little was left on one's plate, the food kept coming. And coming.

Rand made small talk to the diners in his vicinity. Questions were simple. Polite. Those who knew the details of how he was there hid it, Rand imagined, as those who didn't were shrewd enough to stay away from the question.

Despite the easeful warming of the wine, Rand made a concerted effort to play the dinner as the dancing bear, a harmless clown, their monkey on a chain. Anything to disarm them. Perhaps then he still could discover a way to escape. A bit of information from loose lips? A slip of the tongue? A show of the cards, perhaps? Keep them relaxed, he told himself. Misdirection. Then spring when the moment is right. A good linebacker always knows when to blitz.

He played the part.

"So where did you go to school Rand?"

"Bearington Heights, a small school in Virginia."

"Ah, not a Harvard man like your grandfather. I imagine he was upset."

"Kind of. I was accepted to Harvard, but only on my grandfather's connections. But that was okay, I wouldn't have fit in anyway."

The odd pause, then, "What did you study in college?"

"The most worthless of endeavors – English Literature."

Laughter.

"Dr. Lightfoot might disagree with you," said one of the guests.

Hope dropped her head.

"You know, she's cross trained in science quite impressively, but still stands as our foremost authority in the humanities here."

"Oh, yes, I'm aware of that. A lady of many talents," Rand said, then turning to her. "Our resident Lady Macbeth."

Awkward silence. The words out too quick. No thought prior. Rand cursed the wine, caught his fumble and recovered quickly.

"Actually, I miss discussing literature working with a bunch of dumbed-down journalists. Seriously, Hope, excuse me, shall I say, Dr. Lightfoot, who are your favorite authors?"

"I like…so much, it is hard to pin down."

"Oh, come on, don't give us the politic response. You aren't running for office," he offered a quick grin to his dinner guests, the false confidence of the wine continuing its ascent. "Who?"

"Jane Austen."

"Good lord," Rand almost spat out his wine at the remark. "Serious! That sentimental nonsense. Overloaded adjectives, adverbs and predictable romantic garbage, I - " his voice raising, then sensing the embarrassment rising in her cheeks, loathed himself, his cockiness, his self-congratulatory remarks at the table. He inwardly ridiculed himself for putting her on the spot, though in some place in his heart, he felt like she deserved it in the wake of the afternoon's events.

"Excuse me," she said, dabbing her mouth with the edges of the fine linen napkin. She stood and began to walk away.

Rand stood, grabbed her forearm.

"I am –"

He could not finish. She broke away. Made a direct, but unrushed retreat to the back of the room, then through the double doors to the foyer.

"Excuse me," Rand told his audience, their eyes betraying eagerness for more of his antics. "I've been an ass."

He jaunted down the aisle, apathetic to the eyes following him, discarding any thought for ceremony or conduct.

Bursting through the doors, he saw her off to the right, sitting on a bench. But this wasn't a Jane Austen novel. She wasn't gazing out the window looking at the dark night or moonlit mountains. She wasn't crying or clutching a silk handkerchief. She was staring at him with blazing eyes full of anger.

"Hope," he began again.

"You haughty son of a bitch. Are you happy now that you've upset me? Was that your plan? Mr. Charming Bullshit, then needling me in front of my colleagues. You know I've had a trying day, then this? Really – "

"Hope," he tried again. She cut him off.

"I can't believe this is even happening. You! Embarrassing me? How? You egotistical son of a bitch. I can't believe you. You can't even hold a candle to me. To my discoveries, my pedigree, my degrees – "

"Degrees? Are you freaking kidding me? Degrees?" Rand gave a wry laugh. "Who gives a fuck about degrees? And accomplishments? What, rediscovering something that was lost only to hide it again, to pervert it? And you think that makes you better than me? And your – what did you say – background? No 'pedigree.' You actually said 'fucking pedigree.' Pedigree is the most overrated word in the English language. It is also condescending and elitist as hell. I would expect more from you. You don't have any old Mayflower genes in you or even the faux Southern gentry bullshit stock I had to deal with growing up. Dress it up all you want, but you've got Middle America written all over you. And you talk to me about pedigree."

"Leave me alone Rand. We aren't friends. I don't even know you. And I really don't want to. Kent wants me to be your confidante or something. I need to find out what you know, but I don't have to put up with you. I was doing it as a favor."

Her honesty disarmed him. She stood. Turned. He grabbed her arm again. A stern look from one of the footmen stationed near the door in the foyer.

"Hey," then pulling her close to him, he lowered his head and whispered "Please, you've got to help me. Seriously. I have no idea what I'm doing here. I have no idea what is going to happen...to me...I could be dead in an hour...I can be your confidante and play the part if that helps you. I can tell you whatever you want, or need. But I need some answers, too. I need some time. I don't know what's going on, but I've got to get some help, to get out of here."

"I don't think I am the right person for this."

"Hope," he fixed a look that had charmed many a woman, but this time it was earnest. "Hope, there is no one else. I'm lost. I don't know why I am here. I don't know what the fuck I am doing minute to minute. Everything has moved too fast. I know you. I know Kent and he scares the hell out of me. I know I've seen two men killed in the last few days. I know I am locked in my room every damn night. I know something is going on here I shouldn't be a part of. I know I don't belong."

She turned her head, his hand still grasping her arm. A wall of silence dropped like a shroud between them. Then lifted.

She turned back to him, grabbed his lapels, pulled him close. Face to face. Stared into his eyes.

"I will do what I can, though I don't know why. But, if we are to do anything, we must be convincing."

"Convincing?"

She gave an imperceptible nod to the red eyes of the cameras tucked into the corners of the foyer. Then yanked him close, their lips touching, lightly, then with urgency. A deep, warm kiss. The taste of wine and salt mingling. Warmth flooded Rand's body. He put his hand at the small of her back. Pulled her closer. Her breasts now touching his chest. His thighs tingling. A swell in his pants. Then she was away. Holding him at arm's length.

"We must go back in," then louder. "You cad! Wait until later."

She gave a coquettish smile. Flushed, he followed. Understood.

Convincing.

CHAPTER THIRTY-EIGHT

"You know we were going to recruit you at one time."

The voice was delivered from Kent. They were in his study again. Sitting in the same chairs. The fire blazing, the drinks full, the lights low, a faint murmur of music in the background, though this time Rand picked it out as Wagner.

"Recruit me?" Rand responded, half-dumfounded, half-intrigued. He had tried to pace himself through the dinner party, but now found the effects of the many glasses of wine creeping on him. His plan had been to accompany Hope to her quarters after dinner ended, but in the melee, he was ushered with Dr.

Virgillius and Cromwell up to Kent's study. Now the quartet sat around the fire, Rand listening to their musings, the exercising of their extensive vocabularies, the flaunting of their accomplishments.

Rand felt like the interloper he was as if he had crashed a sorority party or sneaked his way into an executive session of a subcommittee back in the Georgia Legislature.

"Oh, yes. You were A-1 material. With your father's, your grandfather's and his father's background. A-1. Your DNA was good. Your ancestry was excellent. And we like to keep this - The Organization, in the family. It is too important to risk spreading to outsiders, per se."

Rand said nothing, stared at the painting by Bierstadt above the fireplace, wished he was in the idyllic wilderness bathed in an easeful light. Anywhere but in Kent's study. Trapped. Hemmed in. Virgillius and Cromwell said nothing. Sipped their drinks. A self-satisfied look on Virgillius's face who stared at the ceiling. Cromwell gazing at the fire as if in deep thought. Kent continued his soliloquy.

"Of course, as you know, when your father and mother died, you became, how do you say, damaged goods. We still kept our eye on you through the years, but with your psychological state - your anger, loss of emotional control and bouts of depression - we ruled you out. Of course, your erratic grades, absurd dedication to football and apparent lack of ambition didn't help either…All in all, too unstable… we went in other directions, found more appropriate candidates."

Rand didn't even look his way. His body frozen. His eyes wet. Wet with sadness of his long departed parents, with the frustration that this man who he didn't even know had the gall to bring it up and in that context. And the unsubtle jab at his failure to live up to his academic expectations in high school and college, the lack of focus that possessed him growing up, the maligned life he had tried to lead and how for many years he had, indeed, channeled it all into football before he realized his passion for the sport didn't match his talent. Then the struggles through college. One semester, Dean's List. The next, on the border of getting kicked out. The confusion. The love for his grandparents, yet the deep loss of his parents. The sadness. Yet, he had survived and through a freefall of circumstances, thrived in a setting he never dreamed of working in – a newsroom.

Yet that sadness, that confusion was vetoed by the resentment he felt now. His stomach churned. The familiar black rage beginning to boil.

"And yet strangely, you came to us anyway. Life is funny," amused with his joke, Kent ceded a small chuckle.

Cromwell gazed up at Rand, offered a sympathetic smile in response. The fire spat out a dance of sparks.

Rand could only take so much of the stifling silence.

"Yes, here I am now. Life is…funny. So, great Lord Kent, riddle me this, what's next?"

Now Kent grew silent. A questioning stare fired at Rand's naked sarcasm.

"We have several options. The main question is not, what's next. It is simply, what do we do with you?"

Rand was silent. Was it his turn to answer? Was it a rhetorical question? Was this his last drink?

Misdirection. Misinformation. Action.

This was fight or flight time. Rand avoided any more hesitation. The answer revealed itself and he could not believe his own reply as the words spilled from his mouth.

"Well, I think I could be an asset. An asset to The Organization. As you pointed out yourself, you were going to recruit me at one time. I've had misfortunes, but I've still shown the potential to be elusive and smart as you yourself have said from the experience in Ireland. Granted, I don't hold all the degrees you probably want, but I am more educated than you give me credit for. More education comes from experience and reading books than from classrooms. And I am an O'Neal. I have a good pedigree as you have pointed out yourself."

The room was silent.

Cromwell cleared his throat.

"I think it might be worth a try. He does make a point. And if he has half the brains and gumption Henry did, well I will vouch for him on that alone."

Kent smiled. In the light, Rand could not decipher what type of smile it was. Self-praising? Satisfied manipulation?

"And you, Dr. Virgillius, what do you think of our young man, here? Worth a shot?"

Virgillius seemed to come out of a dream. His eyes averting from the ceiling to the fire.

"I have my misgivings. He is not one of us. He is coming into this…later than usual…He has much to learn. And not just pure knowledge either. He needs to learn to control himself. To separate passion from reason. With the gravity of what we are dealing with, the sheer importance of it, he needs to learn and unlearn. Smart? Perhaps, but he is too emotionally unstable, possesses a distinct lack of self-discipline, and an aversion to authority. I also have identified a tension, a rage in him, a temper and frankly, I don't like him," he said this leveling his gaze directly at Rand.

"A temper? You mean because I stand up for myself? Because I believe in myself. I would hardly call that a temper. I call that being a man. There is absolutely nothing wrong with that and I will not apologize for it," his voice had raised and he imme-diately recognized it, cursing himself.

"See what I mean," said Virgillius, his eyes still focused on Rand. A scientist detached studying a botched experiment. "Thanks for proving my point, Rand. What did you say, Kent? Damaged goods?"

Kent ended any possibility of confrontation be-tween the two.

"Lots to consider here. Too much for a late night, to which I must bid you all adieu. Except for you Rand. Stay for a nightcap."

CHAPTER THIRTY-NINE

" But, is there anything that you took out of the box and hid anywhere? Anything you might have tucked in a locker or left with a friend? Anything besides the map? Say, a key, talisman, another map, anything else?"

Rand knew he was being probed. This was not the friendly conversation that Kent acted like it was. Which probably meant they had not found everything they expected in his grandfather's box.

"Not that I can think of," Rand said, his mind playing hopscotch between non-chalant conversation and the animalistic instinct of self-preservation. "But, I don't know," he lied. "Everything happened so fast."

"Ah, well, we can keep looking, keep searching. The discovery today is the main thing. I was just hoping you might be able to help us some more. Knowledge is such a key to our work. And your grandfather was a masterful caretaker of it as you have no doubt discovered."

Rand's turn.

"I still don't understand all of this power, this knowledge, whatever you call it. If it is so good, why are you so obsessed with having a monopoly on it?"

"Have you not heard a word I've said since you've been here?" now an edge in Kent's voice.

"Yes, I have. I just supposed there would have been another term to define your mission than good. I mean, if it is so good, why is all of this hidden? Protected? Exclusive? Maybe greed is the right word?"

"Are you saying we have grown greedy?"

"But isn't greed what this place is about? Control. Total ownership. A monopoly on power. On controlling things. Isn't that what you want?"

"Sometimes what we want and what we need are two different things."

"Ah, but who is playing God now?"

"Boy," and Kent leaned on the word. Harsh repetition. "Boy, if you knew the whole story, you would be worshipping me as a minor deity instead of throwing your worthless altruistic notions at me. But, for now, I will forgive you for your ignorance. But, I will also bid you a good night before you drive me to fury and regret."

The dancing blue of Kent's eyes was gone. A steel hardness now. Rand didn't even bother to finish his pint. Gently set it down.

"You can see your way out."

And so he did.

CHAPTER FORTY

He took the elevator back to the main floor and stepped out. Debated his next move. Heard voices drifting up from the banquet hall, the sloppy laughs and pronouncements from the pompous mouths fed on wine and whiskey. He thought about venturing downstairs again. Perhaps he could scout out the castle, fall in with a group of revelers that would give him an extra glimpse about the place. Spy escape routes. At least get another glass of wine to numb his head which was spinning from Kent's words and not the alcohol. He was on the verge of doing that, when a hand grabbed his arm.

He spun around. His eyes met Hope's.

A look of bemused surprise on her face as she saw Rand.

"There you are," a sultry hook in her voice. "I was waiting on you and had just given up. I decided to walk the halls one more time and then...here you are."

Her lilting speech definitely gave away the fact that she had been indulging in the wine selection.

"Here I am."

"Where have you been?" she kept her hand on his arm, but pulled him closer. Gone was the serious stride of the academic, now replaced by a sultry vixen, a hip-swaying saunter.

"Been in Kent's study...talking and such..."

"So new here and yet so highly regarded. I haven't even been up there."

"Not much to see, I'm afraid."

"Oh, you are a good poker player."

He gave a sad grin.

"Come on. Let's go back to my quarters. I have some wine and we can talk privately."

CHAPTER FORTY-ONE

She may have been tipsy, but there was no sloppiness to her passion. Rather, it was focused. Pointed. Bordering on severe. And Rand loved every second of it. The door had just closed behind them, when she turned and embraced him. Pushing him against the door. Her erect nipples piercing through her flimsy blouse against his chest. His senses delightfully overwhelmed by the warmth of her breath on his neck and in his ear, her shallow breathing and her thick hair that, unbound, washed over his eyes. He inhaled her. Her scent filling his nose.

Tongues wrestling, they urgently pulled at each other's clothes, hands greedily grabbing as they made their way through a sitting room to her bed-room. She led him to the bed, fingers unbuttoning his shirt and he half-collapsed on top of her. But she switched positions. Clearly wanted to be on top. Some animalistic impulse writhing through her. She straddled him, frantically ripping his belt off, yanking his pants down. Pulled her dress over her head, breasts swelling. And then he was inside of her. She threw her hair back, and deliberately posed for him, let him admire her body. Then, her hips grinding into him. His hands cupping her supple breasts, exploring her smooth hips. He watched her face in the half light. They moved together. Ebbing and flowing. She bit her lower lip. A small groan escaping her mouth.

CHAPTER FORTY-TWO

He had been awake for over half an hour, feigning sleep, his mind devising plans, envisioning scenarios, more pieces of illumination surfacing.

He felt the bed shift, felt her rise, heard her tiptoeing in the room. A door close. The faint sound of water running from a faucet. A few barely audible coughs. The smell of coffee.

He left the bed, picked up what clothes he could find, a sock here, a crumpled shirt there. Opened the door. Found himself in a small, but smart, sitting room. She was walking out of the kitchen, a cup of coffee in each hand. A flimsy robe barely hiding her upper thigh, her toned legs underneath, her hair pinned up in a bun, exposing her neck. He took it all in, knew he could watch her forever. He hated to spoil the moment with words.

"Hey, sleepyhead," she said.

"Good morning," he said, accepting the extended cup.

They sat on a couch. Sipping the coffee. Her legs curled under her. Rand slightly bent forward. Both silent. Both wondering what the other was thinking. The soreness of the love making ripe in their limbs, the conversation quieted by caution.

Finally Rand spoke.

"I really enjoyed last night."

A faint blush on her cheeks. She lifted her cup to half hide her face, whispered, "me too."

Rand hated to break the blissful peace of the moment. Wanted to soak it in as much as possible, but he could not put it off any longer.

"Hope, I've made up my mind. I want to join."

His words were delivered flat. A matter-of-fact.

Hope stopped in mid-sip. Her back straightened. Waited.

"Sorry if I startled you. I just woke up and there it was. Just there. On my mind. In my heart. A revelation after sleep. Tip of the tongue, you know? The right thing to do. First thought, best thought. I want to be part of this."

A wince across her face. Then a change. A soft hand on his cheek.

"Was I that convincing last night? I don't think I said anything about joining, did I?" her eyes half-lowered, a mischievous grin playing on her face.

"Actions speak louder than words," he countered, his fingers slipping inside her bathrobe, cupping one of her breasts, the smooth skin and warmth spreading through his fingers, a quick stiffening and lightening. Then he stopped. Removed his hand. Remembered what he had to do.

"No, it is the right decision. This is the right time. I need to go see Kent this morning. Should I just go to his room or call or – what is the best way to contact him?"

She pulled back. A coldness descended. The warm flirtation evaporated between them. Cinched her robe close.

"Um, you don't exactly get in touch with Kent. He usually gets in touch with you. But I imagine you could show up. You have a special in like we don't… He seems to like you."

He doesn't like me at all, thought Rand. He just wants to use me.

An hour later, filled with a pot of coffee and freshly showered, Rand was in the elevator ascending to Kent's study. Hope had left while he was in the shower without a goodbye. But, she was right about seeing Kent. All it took was a question posed to a guard walking the corridor who whispered something into his headset and without any wait Rand had been ushered to the elevator and on his way to meet the director.

CHAPTER FORTY-THREE

"Ah, I see." Kent said, studying his fingernails. "Well, what do I need to do? Should I write my grandmother a final note or will the hospital just phone her and tell her I've died? I imagine my belongings will all be donated, right? That's fine, there is nothing there of much importance anyway, just some sentimental items from college. Could I at least will a few items to some friends? If not, that's fine. And what about my – "

"Enough," Kent raised his hand, then withdrew it to his forehead like he had a headache coming on. "You're getting far ahead of yourself, Rand. Slow down."

"Slow down? But, I thought we operated fast. Quick. Efficient. Like with the car accident and the contractor from Liverpool. When I commit to something, I commit 100 percent. I am ready to join The Organization."

"Okay. Let me get to work. I need to make a few calls. And, first things first, I need you to go visit Dr. Virgillius."

"Virgillius? What for exactly?"

"Oh, just a screening, a test for initiates. Part of our process. Merely, a formality of sorts."

"Okay. When?"

"Now. He's waiting for you."

"Waiting for me?"

"Oh, yes. I expected you today. See yourself out. Go back to the first floor. I'll have someone meet you at the elevator and escort you to his lab."

CHAPTER FORTY-FOUR

The elevator whisked open and Rand was met with the face of the man whom he had fought with in Drumcliffe. Was he named Eric? Was that what he remembered? He felt his heart sink. Damn.

"Hello pup. Making yourself at home, eh?" the man took a deridingly cordial tone and placed a beefy hand on Rand's shoulder.

"Good to see you again, too." Flat sarcasm delivered.

"Hey, no hard feelings. I was just doing a job the last time we met. Follow me," they began walking toward a door that led into one of the many court-yards. "How's the ankle?"

"Actually good, thanks."

"Yep, they do a fantastic job here with their sports medicine. Cutting edge shit – transfusions, gene replacement therapy, everything. Can you imagine if the NFL got a hold of this stuff? Those poor bastards would be playing 30 games a year."

"Yeah, that would be great," the shock wearing off. "Yeah, great, actually."

"Yeah, wouldn't it? Thirty plus games a year. No baseball. No women's soccer. No tennis. No golf or cricket. Just football. All year."

"Your name? Eric, isn't it? You played?"

"Yep. I'm Eric. And I did play. Tight end. Division 2. A small college you never heard of. Enjoyed it, though. Free education, lots of girls and kept me in shape," he said.

The sun broke from a cloud as they crossed the courtyard, the light giving both of them a jolt after spending all morning in the dimly-lit corridors. Rand took his time walking a few paces behind Eric. He was eyeing the foreign plants lining the stately beds, the flagstones in idyllic order, the systematic symmetry of it all. Strange smells permeating the air, too. And one familiar. The scent of lemon bit his nose. Another shock to rouse his senses.

"Lemon trees in Austria? Is that what I smell?"

"Yep, crazy, huh?" Eric motioned to a medium-sized tree in the middle of the courtyard sitting high in a bed of mulch. "Apparently some of the doctors are proponents of aromatherapy and they bet a guy in botany he couldn't create a hybrid to handle the Austrian winters. You can see who won the bet."

"How do they taste?"

"Don't know. Don't like lemons, but we go through a ton of lemonade every summer."

Rand admired the tree. The odor was piercing, strong, yet pleasant. Fat yellow globes swung on the branches. The branches were not fragile or brittle like most fruit trees, but extremely thick almost like an oak or poplar.

"What type of tree did they cross breed it with? Looks like oak or some type of beech maybe."

"No idea, pup. Above my pay grade. Come on, let's go."

Rand followed him toward a metal gate at the end of the courtyard. The gates swung open automatically leading them into a similar courtyard. Odd-looking trees and colorful, almost oversaturated colored shrubs lined the edges. More exotic scents pierced the air.

Rand followed Eric toward a building at the end of the terrace where a pair of wooden doors waited for them.

"This is like a bad M.C. Escher painting. Let me guess, we go through those doors into another courtyard."

Eric smiled, but offered no response. Rand noticed the faint words etched in stone above the doors:

sine timore

Eric pushed one of the doors open. Rand was greeted with a white hallway. A row of fluorescent lights overhead gave the corridor a sickly, clinical look. A few closed black doors lined the walls. At the end, a single elevator stood sentry.

"Time for another ride, pup. Let's go down to see the devil," a wry smile

The doors opened. Eric punched in level -13.

"Good lord, everything underground here?"

Eric gave him another wry smile.

"You can figure that out if you're half as smart as they say you are. Satellites see only the surface of things. And the people working the satellites, well, we give them what they want. Nothing but a bunch of genial old scientists puttering around an ancient castle."

The elevator gently bounced to a halt. Doors opened. At the end of another alabaster hall, a vivid red door greeted them.

"Hard to miss this, huh?" Rand offered.

No response.

The door slid open as they approached. Inside the same lack of color. A single desk. White. A computer.

White. No logo. White walls coated in a type of coating that faintly shined. Smooth. The only thing of color in the room was Dr. Virgillius sitting behind the desk. His swarthy face accented by the surroundings and the bland lab coat that clung to his wiry frame.

"Rand." Not a question. A statement. An observation.

"Virgillius." Rand replied, staring at him and then, before he could help it, he turned around. "Eric" then pointing, "Chair. Desk. Computer. Door. Walls -"

"Enough," Virgillius interrupted. "Always the class clown. Never the class act." No anger. Emotionless. Studying. "Shall we begin?"

"Sure."

The blow to his kidney caught Rand completely off guard, lightning strikes up and down his back and he was doubled over, trying to catch his breath. The only sound he could hear was the blood rushing in his ears as he gulped for breath. He began straightening up, his hand on his lower back. Eric circled him, grabbed him by the hair and raised him to eye level.

"Still learnin,' pup. Still learnin.' Rule number one. Always be on guard." And then a backhand from a gloved fist.

"Rule number two, don't forget rule number one."

Rand was turned around and thrown against the wall. He clung to it like a man on a rock face, its coating sticking to his face.

"Well, how do you feel, Rand?" Virgillius said.

How do I answer this, Rand thought? His cheek in flaming pain. His mind reeling. How do I answer this? It is such a stupid question. I feel pain? I feel great? I feel sublime? I feel nothing? Do they want reaction? Regret? Shock? Anger?

Silence.

"Hit him again."

Eric spun him around. The blow this time was not a backhand. Not a bitch slap to taunt him, but a true uppercut delivered at full speed. Rand's head snapped back and he fell back into the wall. Then half-slouched down. Coughed. His entire face numb from the blow. Tiny stars bursting in his vision. He half-saw Eric walking toward him.

"Again." Virgillius said.

Rand raised his hand above his head, his body still slumped against the wall.

"Wait," between gasps, "Wait...wait...okay, okay. What do you want?"

"A simple answer, Rand. An answer you could have given me the first time. How do you feel?"

Rand dared to push himself up. Looked at Virgillius. Eric beside him. Gloved hands fisted.

"I feel dazed. I feel pain. I feel confusion."

"Dazed. Confused. Yes. Pain. Yes. How about anger? Do you feel anger, Rand?"

"Uh," the right answer, what is the right answer? "Yes, I do feel anger."

"More, Rand. More."

"I feel anger. Angry at you. Angry at Eric. We were just riding the fucking elevator, talking football in the courtyard. Now, what the hell is this! God damn right I'm angry!"

"Enough," a hand lifted from Virgillius. "Good. This is where you need to stop. These are the situations where you need to divorce your emotion and your reason. All situations should be met with logic and clarity. Creativity and enlightenment will come. But on the outset, nothing but logic. Logic and obedience. No need to cloud our judgment. No false ideas of morality, of passion, of sympathy. Do you understand?"

"Yes."

"Good. Sit."

Rand cautiously walked to the chair. Hesitated.

"Do you not trust me, Rand?"

"Why should I?"

A smile on the stone face.

"Good. Now you're using reason. You can't trust me. You have no reason to. Understand. But I promise I will not have Eric hit you again if you are honest with me."

Rand hesitated, then began edging himself into the chair.

"How do you feel now, Rand?"

"Still angry. Confused...vulnerable."

"Very astute. Vulnerable. I like that. You are verbose, if nothing else. How would you normally react in this situation?"

"Well, I'm usually not in a situation like this. I mean this isn't what I do on the weekends, I –"

"Enough with the wit, Rand. If you're serious about your induction, then act like it. Be it. I ask how you would normally react to this. This situation of being assaulted for no reason. Two men in a room. Weaponless...I hear you were once a decent athlete. Your reaction?"

"How would I react?" Rand asked aloud, his mind still reeling, the genesis of a headache forming. "I would probably want to beat the shit out of you both. I might make a lunge for the chair or the computer. Try to knock one of you with it and then make a dash for the door. Of course, the door is probably locked by some code or unseen camera so I would be left to fight one of you. Knowing my luck it would be Eric. Eric probably has a weapon on him, so I would be fu- uh, excuse me, no match for him."

"Ah, Rand. Not a very good answer. Not thought out. Still lacking total reason. And too much emotion. Way too much emotion. The fighting, the running. The typical fight or flight, a terrible instinct in our species."

"Okay. What would you do?"

"Let's see," a slight pause. "Who can get you out of this room? Probably me? Correct. As a senior member here, I would have more access to our facility than Eric. You could hit Eric. Wouldn't do too much good. He is expertly trained as you have noticed."

A smile on Eric's face. Virgillius continued.

"What would I do then? Try to take me hostage. Use anything as a way to threaten me, to harm me. A neck hold to choke me, a pen or pencil to stab me in the carotid artery. You threaten to end my life with a simple jab of a pen in the right place. Then use me as a means to your end. A bargaining chip, a hostage. I will open the door. Eric would not hurt me. See, thinking instead of reacting. Logic. See, I thought this through. Started at the end and thought back to the beginning. No random violence. No running and animalistic impulses and that nonsense. Simple reason. Reason, Rand, is everything. Reason."

He let the word hang there.

"Does that make sense to you, Rand?"

"Yes."

"Good. Now another test. Eric," he turned to the guard. "Empty your weapons on my desk."

"Sir?" a look of confusion.

"Empty your weapons on my desk. As a senior member of this organization I should not need to repeat myself, should I?"

"No sir."

Eric withdrew a knife that was strapped to the side of his pants, a wicked looking dagger from inside his shirt, then bending down, reached underneath his pants leg and withdrew a Glock pistol. He laid them all on the table.

"Quite well armed isn't he, Rand?"

"Yes."

"You see, we are all prepared, but we don't like our staff to see us toting guns about, do we Eric?"

"No sir," Eric replied, confusion still on his face, but the words spilling out mechanically.

Virgillius picked up the Glock, turned it over in his hand.

"Not my favorite handgun. Blocky, crude, but effective and copied by everyone. However, it lacks a certain finesse to it. But it does its job doesn't it, much like Eric."

He turned and handed the gun to Rand.

"Now Rand. Shoot him."

CHAPTER FORTY-FIVE

The words spun through his head.
Shoot him.

Then the other phrases. The old phrases, the phrases his grandfather had embedded in him. The phrases he had to keep repeating to himself.

Take stock of the situation, use forced direction, then misdirection, think before you act, and when you act, act swiftly. And, short term sacrifice for the long term goal. Self-preservation. Improvise. Live to fight another day. Use forced direction, then misdirection

He kept repeating it to himself as if the very words could change him. Could justify what he had done.

But, none of it really mattered.

All words.

Nothing concrete.

Nothing to stand up and measure oneself against. The fact was simple: He had killed Eric. Shot him. And then at Virgillius's urging, shot him again. And again. And again. And again. Until the magazine emptied. Don't worry about the mess, Virgillius had said. The cleaning staff will take care of that. The off-handed remark as he took the pistol back from Rand. Well done, he had said. Now go get cleaned up. Here's a pill to help you settle and focus for our next session. Rand had taken the pill, feigned a swallow and lodged it on the roof of his mouth. Now as he was being whisked up in the elevator, the smell of gunpowder and blood on his shirt, he faked a cough and spat it into his hand. Shoved his hand in his pocket. No doubt there could be cameras in the elevator. The door opened and he briskly walked back to his room. Avoided all eyes from those passing him. Undressed. Let the warm water of the shower try to wash away his guilt. Struggled to push back the tears, but they cascaded down his face, mixing with the water, his unspeakable shame, before sinking into the drain.

CHAPTER FORTY-SIX

The knock on the door came as he was tucking in his shirt, the damp from the shower still in his hair. Damn, they are efficient if nothing else, he thought.

"Yes?"

"Mr. St. James would like to see you as soon as you are dressed. Would you care for a drink beforehand?"

Clear head. Clear head. Clear head. But not too clear.

"I think I will wait until I get to his study, I do not want to be late."

"As you wish."

The invisible voice sailed away.

CHAPTER FORTY-SEVEN

K ent was in one of the chairs in front of a small fire.

"Come in, come in," he said rising, a cheerful lilt to the words.

Rand walked toward him.

"Take a seat. I've already got your drink poured."

Rand was not surprised. The perfect pint of Guinness. Wanted to refuse, but felt he had to play the part. He sat. Sipped. Lit up a cigarette from a pack he kept in his pocket. The smoking. The drinking. Becoming all too routine now. Convenient gentlemen drugs used to constantly ease off the edge.

"Virgillius told me you passed this morning with flying colors. Well done."

"Thank you." Rand forcing the words out. Harder than any lies before.

"We were both a bit worried. Virgillius more than me. He thought we might have a situation. You running amuck with a handgun. Maybe even killing him," a dry laugh, "But I knew. I knew I could count on you. I know a dark horse when I see one."

Rand didn't respond.

"But then, you didn't take the pill afterwards. Tsk-tsk, a real shame. That was your only failure on the test."

Rand was quiet again. No denial. No affirmation.

"How do I know?" Kent asked.

Rand was beginning to tire of Kent's continued rhetorical questions. The questions he used repeatedly to prop himself up and boost his esteem.

"Simple. If you had taken it, you would be asleep by now and we would be monitoring your brain waves to see how your synapses, adrenaline and such responded to the incident. I can't blame you for not taking it, but if we are going to trust you with a handgun, the least you can do is indulge us with a pill."

Rand stammered. "I, I'm sorry. I was – not afraid – I was, apprehensive. You're right, though. Should I take it now?"

"No, quite all right. You can undergo all that later. I've got another surprise for you today."

Rand forced the words out. Did not feel them coming from his throat, but almost saw himself saying it as if from a great height far away.

"Another surprise. I can't wait."

CHAPTER FORTY-EIGHT

"You know I can't drop you off at the spot of the discovery, right?"

The words burst through the static into Rand's headphones.

"What?"

"I have to drop you off a ways back. Sorry. Orders. Apparently this latest work zone is highly sensitive to electric equipment and I don't want to die in this bird."

"Understand. Thanks."

"Yeah, your radio and everything you need is in the backpack we loaded. Make sure to take it with you."

Rand was in the helicopter as it swooped over a cluster of firs on a return trip toward the site where Weston had been shot. Besides the pilot, he was alone. He imagined he could kill the pilot and fly the chopper to safety. But, first of all, he had never flown anything. Secondly, he was still in a half-daze from the morning's murder. And, as self-loathing as he found it, he was curious as to what the discovery held. What would the stone look like? What type of energy would be emanating from it? If it was strong enough to unhinge Weston, strong enough to affect the workings of a helicopter, would people around it begin losing their minds as well? Would there be protective gear? How would it be transported back? Truck? Helicopter? All thoughts were interrupted by the voice of the pilot.

"Hot load off, again. You remember, right?"

Rand nodded. A few minutes later he was walking through the forest in what he thought was the right direction when a generic phone ring emanated from his backpack. He unzipped and grabbed a satellite phone.

"Hello."

"Rand. Good afternoon." It was Hope's voice.

"Afternoon."

"I see you're heading in the right direction. Continue about another quarter mile directly up the slope and you'll see an ATV about 100 yards to your left, roughly north by northwest. Keys are in it. Take it and drive about a mile further up. You should be able to see our camp from there. Someone will meet you."

"But, what? You can see I am heading –"

"I got to go. See you soon. Bye."

They must really trust me, Rand thought. He knew he had paid a steep price for trust. He was still reconciling himself with killing Eric. A wave of guilt washed over him again. He didn't know Eric. The man had not been his friend. But he had done it. Had squeezed the trigger. For what? To survive to live another day. Even another hour. Time. He needed time to formulate a plan, to escape. And he needed access. He had to get further inside The Organization. But at what price would he relinquish giving up the facade?

He tried to shrug off the guilt of playing this second life by pushing his boots into the soil and increasing his speed up the ridge. Feeling the burn in his thighs and the sun on his skin helped ease the burden, but the dark wave still lingered in his mind, clouded his thoughts.

Then there it was. The ATV. The keys in it. A half tank of gas. Water bottles and a stash of granola bars in one seat.

It roared to life and he drove it up the slope.

CHAPTER FORTY-NINE

A colossal white dome constructed of an unknown material dominated the clearing where
the piece had been found.

Surrounding it were a half-dozen ATVs, a small
white tent suited more for summertime soirees rather than scientific endeavors and several shipping
containers modified with windows and doors. More
than a dozen antennas and satellite dishes stood at
attention in a cluster about 40 yards away. As Rand
turned off the ignition and coasted to a stop, a guard
appeared from some concealed area wearing the traditional black uniform, an Uzi in his hand.

"Rand O'Neal?"

"Yes."

Cautious. This would be a good place for a killing, he thought. Plenty of places to discard the body and apparently the people who worked at The Organization had no issue with murder.

"Good. I.D. card please?"

Rand unclipped the badge from his shirt, handed it over. The guard looked at it for a moment. Unclipped a satellite phone from his belt.

"Dr. Lightfoot. I've got Rand O'Neal out here. Should I send him to the safety station or do you want to escort him direct?"

Hope's voice came through.

"We're taking a break so I'll come out and take him direct. Thank you."

Rand sat on the ATV and waited, closed his eyes, enjoying the sunlight on his face. He did not attempt any small talk with the guard, his desire for additional conversation wilted by the morning's actions. Fifteen minutes later, Hope appeared.

"Good afternoon, Rand."

"Good? Maybe. Afternoon? Already?"

"Yes, you look a little pale. Have you eaten?"

"No."

"Follow me. I'll get you something to eat and we'll get you processed."

CHAPTER FIFTY

The grandiose meals at the castle were non-existent outside its walls. Rand wolfed down a utilitarian meal of a soggy sandwich, bottled water and a protein bar. Hope looked at him with a half-grin.

"Not exactly wild boar is it? Then again, we're here to work. We'll celebrate later."

Rand was sitting on a folding table in the white tent he had spied when he arrived. Around him were a half dozen more tables and chairs, coolers and cots. Thick curtains bordered on each side, offering a small block against the breeze.

Rand crunched the last of the granola bar, washed it down with a warm swig of water.

"All done?" Hope asked.

Rand nodded.

"Good, take this," she handed him a shiny red pill.

"What is this?" Rand asked.

"Potassium Iodate. Basic radiation shield, but in a much larger dosage than you can find on the market, plus with a few specialized supplements and minerals that work well. And don't worry, the chance for any exposure to radiation is nil. We just like to be prepared for, er, other chemicals in the environment and this has a similar chemical make-up to fend off any poisoning. But enough, follow me, there is work to do."

CHAPTER FIFTY-ONE

S he led him to a slim windowless trailer, like an
elongated Jetstream.

"Are we going camping, Dr. Lightfoot?"

No humor on her face now. No trace of the night
before. The time devoted to the wrestling of limbs
and twisting of sheets. The grinding hips against
his, her open mouth above him flashed through his
mind once. A quick fleeting image jettisoned by her
next sentence.

"No. The potency of the stones can be very, very
powerful. You saw what happened to Weston. If we
do not take precautions and extreme protection
extracting it – well, the power it emanates is severe
enough to drive you insane."

"I saw that, remember?"

She ignored him, slid the door open.

Rand followed her. Inside, the trailer was barren except for a row of what appeared to be slimmed-down space suits hanging on hooks. Rand fingered the material. It was a foreign fiber. Almost a flexible fiberglass or a lighter grade aluminum.

"Stop!" Hope slapped his hand away. "We wear these to keep any particles off of us. We don't want to expose ourselves afterwards by rubbing them."

"Sorry, sorry. Easy. I just was curious."

"It's okay. They've been de-contaminated, but still, we always put gloves on first. I don't want to risk it."

"You mean you don't want to risk it happening to me."

A faint blush. A turn of the head.

"Here," she said, donning a pair of gloves. "Let me help."

She slipped a pair of gloves on his hands, then the suit. It was light and incredibly flexible. She pulled a string on his sleeve and it shrunk to conform to his body.

"Goodness," he said. "Very efficient, but not flattering if you're on the heavy side."

Finally, she acquiesced a smile.

"Take this," she handed him a helmet that resembled an astronaut's headgear, but was sleeker and less bulky.

"There are tiny filters on each side for breathing. You'll be fine. Our concern is more with physical contact, than with airborne particles. You also have built-in headphones so you can hear everything."

"And, let me guess, a microphone so everyone can hear us, too, right?"

She nodded. Rand watched her don a similar suit and followed her out a hermetically-sealed door.

CHAPTER FIFTY-TWO

The inside of the dome was brightly lit. Rand could see now it was not a permanent structure, but rather a pre-fabricated building that could be assembled quickly when needed. A row of portable air conditioning units similar to the types he had seen on the sidelines of football games whispered plumes of cold air that drifted wraith-like to the ground. Workstations were perched around the circumference of the dome; gigantic computer terminals stacked on top of each other like miniature skyscrapers, multi-split TV screens, digital seismic monitors, barely audible generators, real time weather beaming on the tent's walls and 3-D images projected into the air itself.

Beyond the rabbit hole again, Rand thought.

In the middle of the room was a pit. Tremendously wide. Rand could see nothing in its guts but blackness. Above it hovered a machine that resembled a giant, steel spider. Tentacles spread out from its black underbelly, six long legs supported it. Extending from its sides were pincers with all types of tools, needles, drills, red-eyed scanners and other apparati that seemed ripped from a science fiction movie. Rand could not see a cockpit or a bubble for manual direction.

"Remote control?" he asked pointing at it.

"We prefer to call it handheld direction, but yes," Hope said.

The man Rand recognized as The Bear was near the edge of the pit holding what appeared to be a Frankensteinian mash-up of a Geiger counter and a metal detector. Rand could hear his voice in his ears, along with several others. They had apparently walked into the middle of some type of argument.

"I tell you, we need to drill deeper first."

Rand did not recognize the voice.

"No, nyet, nyet, nyet!" The Bear emphasized and Rand could see him raise a fist in frustration. "We are too close. Do you want to break the stone like those fools did at Mt. St. Helen's? Do you want a situation like the damn tsunamis we caused in the Pacific? Is that what you want? Do you not remember what havoc that caused? What losses we incurred? Have you learned nothing? Idiots. Idiots. No. This is my operation. I am calling the shots. From now on, we dig by hand."

"That could take all day," the voice again. "Hours, maybe a day, our equipment is better now and I can see on my monitor that we still have several feet at least, I – "

"No. I said no. I do not have time to argue. You are off the operation."

Rand saw movement on the far end of the dome as two guards moved toward a lone man in front of a tower of computers.

"Wait, I – "

The Bear made a cut throat motion with his hand. Rand could not see the man's face, but heard the scream piercing the headphones, watched one of the guards jab a hypodermic needle into his back. The man's body limp. The guards carrying him away.

"Now, let us dig, slowly, carefully."

The Bear's head swiveled. Eyes assessed Rand.

"Dr. Lightfoot. You bring us a guest, I see?"

"Yes," Hope replied. "He is – "

"I know who he is. The one with us yesterday. The fucking Golden Boy, eh? The O'Neal always in Kent's study. Is he here to watch or assist?"

"He is here to watch, to observe."

"But, he could assist, no? Now, we are under-staffed and I need somebody to help with the delicate part. Everyone else," he vaguely motioned with his hand, "is tied up with technology, science, skill work as they call it. But, he could be used to work. To help me dig."

"I don't know," Hope replied. "That might be a bit of a jump for him. I don't know if Kent would approve. He is just learning. He is still ignorant on many of these things. He – "

"Enough. This is my operation. Kent put me here so he could stay comfortable behind his fancy desk," then looking at Rand. "Boy, are you slabby?"

"Pardon me?"

"Are you slabby? Ah, in English then. Are you weak? Are you delicate? Is your God damn arm broken?"

"No."

"Then come, help me work and I might show you things to undo your ignorance."

CHAPTER FIFTY-THREE

The word, 'boy' again. The condescension. Rand would love to drop this Bear off in Techwood or The Bluff neighborhoods in Atlanta with that attitude and see how long he would last. Rand restrained his thoughts and it was no thanks to Virgillius's lecture on reason and emotion, but the gnawing curiosity of what lay below.

He and The Bear were being steadily belayed down, down, down into the semi-darkness. The Bear would occasionally drop something resembling a glow stick to judge their distance and then relay their progress to the people above.

"Slower, we're at 30 feet. Slower, 10 feet. Slower, five feet."

Rand felt perspiration break out on his forehead. His stomach knotted. He waited. Waited for the madness which had permeated Weston to sweep over him at any moment. Wondered if these were his last few moments of sanity, perhaps of life.

"Good, we are here," The Bear said.

Rand's feet touched solid earth.

"You okay, boy?"

Rand nodded.

"Good. You look worried? Worried about Weston, huh? Idiot. Do not be worried. These suits are specifically calibrated to keep us from such fate. It took years, decades, centuries for us to realize the need for this. On the way, many of us died from direct contact or exposure. I can only imagine the poor fools in their pith helmets and layers of robes trying to handle something this big."

"But wait. Kent said y'all – you – were digging up these stones hundreds of years ago. How did they manage that, then?"

The Bear gave another bitter laugh.

"Is that what he told you? Ha, those were shards or smaller stones. This, underneath us, is no shard. It is quite big, according to our data. A whole piece intact. About the size of your American football. Tremendous. Probably not as big as the one we found last year in the Pacific, but big enough. And it is not always size that matters, eh? And can you believe we were blind enough to not even see it in our own backyard?" The Bear shook his head. "So blind. But thanks to your friend Dr. Lightfoot, we were able to find it. Fucking Mozart, huh? Mozart, a melodic baby compared to my Stravinsky. Bullshit music. Simple fucking chords. But enough of this talk. You can feel smart later talking to Kent at headquarters, but now I need you to help me. Unlock your carabiner. Turn on the light located at the top of your helmet."

Rand lifted his hand and switched the knob. A wide swath of halogen light illuminated the small chamber. The Bear did the same.

"Now," The Bear said. "Now, comes the delicate part. We will dig. Using our hands like fucking primates, like God damn gorillas."

The Bear dug his hands into the earth and began to move it piece by piece, scooping it out, the dark soil dirtying his white suit. Rand began to do the same.

"Remember, slow. You could probably touch it and be fine, but precaution is everything. That is why we do not even use trowels or shovels."

One hour. Two hours. The two used their hands to dig around the pit, every 30 minutes or so The Bear called for a bucket to be lowered and dirt was taken up to the top.

Rand was scraping the soil away. The work was not painstakingly hard, but tedious. He had begun to grow bored, the adrenaline giving way to a post-endorphin haze. It was getting warm inside the suit. Inside the belly of the earth. Then he saw it. A faint blue light beneath his hands. He scraped away another layer of dirt. The light grew brighter. Shimmering. The entire chamber lit up with its luminosity.

A shout in his ears.

"Stop! No more digging. We have it!"

CHAPTER FIFTY-FOUR

I t was stunning.
A shimmering turquoise. Or was it topaz? Silver?
Cobalt? Rand couldn't tell. The stone shifted in its
color. Not exactly glowing, but subtly changing, like
a sky eclipsed by fast moving clouds, throwing a variety of shades of color onto the walls of the hole.

Rand was stunned not only at the beauty, but
also how small it was. The Bear had told him it was
the size of an American football, but still, after hearing how big the discovery was, he had automatically
assumed it would be more substantial in proportion.

And then there was a sensation. Rand had
felt it initially, but dismissed it to adrenaline or

psychosomatics. But, now he was sure. He could feel something. Slightly electrifying. His senses sharpened. Wired. Like drinking too much coffee when he was 13. Like the air ripe before a summer thunderstorm. Tension. But, an alertness, too. A vivid alertness.

"Are you okay, boy?"

Rand looked at The Bear. Saw the man's glistening face through his helmet's shield. Sweat pouring down his forehead, a pale sheen, his eyes blinking rapidly.

"I'm fine, I guess, just a little wired, a little tight if that makes sense." Rand said. "I almost feel good. How are you?"

"I – I am fine," then shaking his head. "No, nyet, not okay. I need to go up for a breather, I –" The Bear slumped backwards against the rough-hewn earth. Rand ran over, grabbed his arm, tried to hold him upright as his body slid down the wall.

"Hold on, Hold on. Hey," Rand shouted. "Hey, we need some help down here. Now! Are you listening? Is anyone listening?"

"What kind of help, exactly," a monotone voice from above, crackling with static, "We need more specifics. I need to speak to The Bear."

"Just shut up, I'm hooking The Bear back onto his cable. You need to get him up and out of here now. He is very sick, something is wrong."

Rand found the carabiner on the floor, clicked it to The Bear's suit, then felt the man tug at his arm. Rand looked into his eyes, they were glossy and unblinking.

"You're going to be okay," Rand said. "Just take it easy."

"It is strong, isn't it?" the voice a bit clearer now, less weak.

"What?"

"The stone. I can feel it. It is strong. Very strong. I – I did not know."

"Yeah, sure. But, hey, hang in there. We're getting you out."

"Are you ready for us to bring him up?" Again the monotone voice through his helmet.

"Yes, we're ready," Rand checked the line once again. "I told you, get him out."

Rand watched The Bear slowly ascending into the light above, his body limp in the drag of the cable.

"Are you okay, Rand?" another voice broke through. It was Hope.

"Sure, I think so. Just a bit wired. I think something is wrong with The Bear, I – "

"Enough," the monotone voice. "We're pulling you out too, O'Neal. Sending in a fresh team. Ready your suit for ascension."

Rand didn't argue. He attached the carabiner to his suit and gave it a jerk. He began to rise, the strange color inside the ground illuminating the walls around him, its color dancing like the flickers of an otherworldly flame.

CHAPTER FIFTY-FIVE

He dined that night with Kent, Cromwell and Virgillius. The four of them in Kent's personal dining room where just a few days ago Rand had met him with a dazed head and a sore ankle.

Now, he sat around a table, his mind a blur of confusion. A guard had been waiting for him on the heli-pad back at the castle and escorted him to Kent's quarters before the whir of the helicopter's blades could even cease. Not even time for a shower or a minute or two of solace.

Everything rushed.

Then dinner. Another decadent feast of lollipop lamb chops, roasted potatoes, an array of kale and "just picked this morning mushrooms," Kent informed them.

"So what did you think of the extraction today, Rand?"

"It was...eventful, insightful, and amazing."

"Yes, amazing, eh? I have not been on a dig in years. Too dangerous for my position now, but I do remember them. I do..." his voice trailed off, and his eyes lost their focus, became dreamy.

Cromwell and Virgillius silently sipped their wine.

"How is The Bear?" Rand asked.

"Oh, he should be fine, I think. He suffered what most do – a reaction of some sort to the stone. You saw it with Weston and, God knows, the three of us here have seen it countless times through the years, I say, once – "

"But, what about the suits?" Rand interrupted. "I thought the suits were engineered to keep all of the rays, the effects, well, whatever they are called at bay."

"We do our best to prepare, to prevent, to ensure the safety of all of our employees, but things happen. Different people react certain ways. Some react barely at all. Some have, uh, distinct innate, genetic advantages. But, The Bear? He fell into another category. He might be fine," at this Kent levelled his eyes at Virgillius. "What do you think, doctor?"

"Perhaps," he spoke flatly, his eyes, focused on the wine glass clasped in his hand. "Perhaps. It will

take a few days and much testing to check his neural patterns, his blood, his very chromosomes. Then
we'll need to run a battery of psychological tests. So,
that said, time will tell."

"Yes, yes," murmured Kent. "But about you, Rand.
Did you feel anything today? You seem to be with us
per se." A question posed as a statement.

"I am fine. I did feel something, though," as
he said this, he felt the full attention of the three
men on him. "It was electric, kind of, a wired-ness, a
sharpness of the senses. But then again maybe it was
just my mind playing tricks on me. Some old fashioned psychosomatic tendencies…."

Rand looked around the table for any approval
or empathy.

Nothing said. Eyes averted.

Kent cleared his throat. A knowing smile.

"No, you summed it up quite well. A sharpness of
the senses. That is a facet of the Slendoc Meridian.
A start, you might say. We deduced as much. We will
probably run some tests on you tomorrow. Nothing
serious, of course, just to compare any potential
anomalies between you and your new Russian friend.
But, enough about that, let's adjourn to the den for
some refreshment."

The quartet moved to the den where the ever-
present fire was blazing.

Rand took his seat. The Guinness. The smokes.
Sighs of satisfaction went up from around the group.

"Well, Rand, how do you feel your training has been going?"

"Fine, I suppose, I mean, it has just started, but -"

"He did well today. Satisfactory," Virgillius interrupted.

Rand involuntarily flinched at the clinical analysis of Eric's killing. Had almost forgotten about it in the post-euphoric digging of the stone.

"Yes, he did. I knew he would," Kent again, the self-assurance. "We've got a class A man with us, I think. Oh, you can't be sure this early, but most of our candidates do not kill on the first assignment, if at all. It takes time to break them down, to wean out their moral superstitions and stipulations. But you, Rand. My God, boy! You really displayed a cold meticulousness I haven't seen in years. The first time! And quite efficient from what the video replay showed me. Level arm. Good aim. No misses. Well done! A class A man."

The shark like smile. A raising of his glass.

Rand felt his stomach tighten. Realized his own stupidity. He did not have to kill Eric after all. It was a test. Damn. How foolish. But how was he to know? He had no guide. No training book. No manual. He was just thinking. Surviving. Damn it. He felt rage gnawing at him. Pushed it down. Willed a smile. Lifted his glass in return to Kent's toast.

"You okay, old boy?" Kent asked.

"Oh, just fine. Just happily surprised to be called a class A man. Not something I've heard much the past several years," he said, giving them the lies he knew they wanted.

Then raised his own glass of wine. Tried to keep his hand from trembling as he took a long drink.

"Oh, yes. Well done," Kent said. "We'll have a few more rounds of training during the next few days, weeks – psychological, physiological, but you're well on your way."

He let the words dangle there. Rand noticed Cromwell stiffen. Virgillius impassive as always.

"Ah, but who knows, one step at a time, right?" Kent asked, expecting no answer, and then picking at a piece of tobacco at the end of his cigarette, "but by God you have come far fast."

CHAPTER FIFTY-SIX

There was no late night session that evening.

Kent did not even offer a round of post-dinner drinks around the fireplace and Rand followed Virgillius and Cromwell's lead as they made exits. He took the elevator to the main floor, went to Hope's room.

He made a few gentle raps on her door, but nothing.

He knocked again, this time with his knuckles, the pounding sounding distinctly loud in the deserted hallway.

He had almost decided she wasn't in or was ignoring him, when he heard a bolt turn. The door marginally opened.

"Hope."

"Hello Rand. How are you?"

"Fine, uh, how are you?"

"Fine." A chilliness in the air. A blandness to the words.

"What are you up to? Do you want to, uh, go for a walk, or…" the words failed him. Was he asking her out for a date? If so, where did one go for a date here? What exactly was he doing? Things had moved so fast, he hadn't had time to think about the surrealness of it all. He just knew, he needed to see her. Needed to find some point of reference, some anchor in this storm for his spinning ship.

"A walk?" she asked.

Rand gave up any pretension.

"Yeah, a walk. I don't know. Let's go sit outside in one of the courtyards, or get a drink. I'm sure this place has a bar of sorts. Or just talk." He wanted to add something more clever, implying a lack of clothes in their talk, but words were failing him.

"I don't know, Rand. I'm pretty exhausted after today."

All her warmth gone. The door still cracked open. Her hands on the frame. No invitation.

"Okay. Well, maybe I'll see you later."

He began walking back down the hall.

"Are you going up to Kent's for another night of secret discussions?" a slight acidity.

"No. To bed."

He turned back around and kept walking, could feel her eyes on the back of his head.

CHAPTER FIFTY-SEVEN

The last of the late summer blue had left the sky, surrendering to the encroaching blackness. A few stars pinpricked the night. Rand stood by the open windows. He was in complete solitude for the first time in days. Just him and his monk cell of a room. Fished a cigarette out of his pocket. Lit it. Blew a plume of blue smoke from his mouth, watched it drift up and dissipate into the night air and tried to think. But, he was tired of thinking. And tired of not having time to think. Had been on his feet, using his wits, taking in so much the past few days, he did not know what it was like to not think. To simply be.

But this was not the time for Zen-like introspection, he knew. He needed to plan. He felt like he was earning their trust. Perhaps they were still using him, but he could use them back. He felt like he was out of any immediate danger. But, then anything could change at any moment. After all, that had been the only constant.

Now, he just needed to think.

The words again. The phrases. His mantra passed on from his grandfather.

Take stock of the situation. Use forced direction, then misdirection, think before you act, and when you act, act swiftly.

CHAPTER FIFTY-EIGHT

Sleep was fleeting. His mind racing between a dozen different scenarios. Things to act on. Things to react to. Somewhere in the dead hours around 4 a.m., the time when deep dreams invade, he finally fell asleep. Restless dreams. Faces of Hope. Of Eric. Of Virgillius. Worry on his mind. But, he had nothing to fret about. No late night raid stormed through his door. He did not wake up in another unfamiliar room.

He woke early, the sun not even casting its yellow rays on the mountain peaks. He sat on the edge of his bed, patiently waiting for the timely knock on his door, the carafe of coffee, the ritual. But there was no tap on the door this morning, no summoning by a maid. He began dressing. Only when he stepped out of the bathroom did he notice the door slightly ajar.

Rand peaked out. Saw an empty hallway.

Went to the Drachen dining room.

The table was empty. Rand sat. Waited. The door to the kitchen opened. One of the non-descript servers came out and saw him in surprise.

"Oh, hello, sir."

'Hello," Rand affected a smile.

"Can I help you, sir?"

"I, uh, was hoping to find some breakfast," he said, patted his stomach.

"Oh, okay. Um, we aren't having any events in here this morning, but I know the cafeteria is open 24 hours a day. They should have something for you."

"Oh, okay. Where is the cafeteria?"

She shot him a curious look.

"Sorry, I'm new here and have only dined in this room."

"Oh, you must be a VIP. Of course. Just go to the elevator. It is on the first floor down. Floor -2. Then follow your nose."

"Thank you."

CHAPTER FIFTY-NINE

If the dining room on the main floor conjured images of European royalty, the cafeteria was the exact opposite. Illuminated by rows of fluorescent lights situated among ceiling tiles, a green hue lit the oblong room. At some tables, groups of scientists clustered, their heads buried in conversation. Other tables just held one or two workers, some had their eyes glued to their laptop, absentmindedly shoveling food into their mouths, others dozed, faces planted in the sleeves of rumpled lab coats. The cafeteria line ran along one corner of the wall. In keeping with the utilitarian theme of the room, it was self-serve.

Rand expected the food to be bland. He was not disappointed. A plateful of runny eggs, limp bacon and brittle toast was washed down by bitter coffee. He sat for a few minutes aftcrwards. Waiting. Waiting for something to direct his day. Should he go see Kent? Try Hope again? Was he being observed? Feeling conspicuous, he was about to make his way up to his room when a voice behind him said, "Mr. O'Neal."

Rand turned to find a short, squat man dressed in a white lab coat. A greasy forehead, toothy smile and bright brown eyes made him a pleasant change among the grim and smug residents he had encountered since his stay.

"Yes."

"Good, we've been looking for you," Rand picked up a slight German accent. "Of course, I always believe the stomachum is the great signpost, so follow your nose and you'll find your man."

"Stomachum?"

"Oh, apologies, I slip into Latin too often. Too much science. Stomachum. The stomach."

Rand nodded.

"I know who you are so I have the advantage. But, who am I?" the man asked Rand, pointing proudly at his chest, the smile again. "I am Dr. Dunkel. I work with Dr. Virgillius. Come, follow me. We have a busy morning."

CHAPTER SIXTY

R and was in Dr. Virgillius's office again. The same one as the day before. There was no trace of the violence. No blood stains, smears, not even a scent of antiseptic pierced the odorless air. Virgillius was sitting in his chair, typing on his computer. He had not acknowledged Rand when he walked in. Dunkel went and stood behind him like a faithful dog, waiting for its master. Still smiling at Rand. Waiting for Virgillius to finish.

"So Rand, how are you today?" Virgillius finally asked, eyes still on the screen.

"Well, besides that marvelous breakfast, I ate, I – "

Rand caught himself, remembered the lesson from yesterday. No more smart ass retorts, he told himself.

"My apologies, Dr. Virgillius. I am fine today, I suppose, though I think 'fine' is a weak description. Candidly, I am nervous. I am apprehensive. I am excited. I am ready to continue my training."

Virgillius finally looked up from his screen. A thin smile on his face.

"An acceptable answer Rand. Rapid improvement. We have a few training exercises for you this morning. Kent has something for you this afternoon, I believe, doing research in The Cavern. But for now, we will need your entire focus here. Can you do that?"

"Yes."

"Good. Follow me."

Virgillius led them down the banal hall to a room similar to the one they had been in before. Instead of a desk and a computer, it had three chairs around a table. All plastic. A projection screen was on one wall and a mirror on the other. Shit, Rand thought, there is where it begins. They will conduct their psychological experiments, then observe. Time to steel myself.

As if reading his thoughts, Dunkel spoke, "Ah, relax, this is not a brainwashing exercise."

Virgillius gave a mirthless laugh.

Rand refrained from shooting back a hate-filled look and instead stared straight ahead.

The laugh again.

"What?" Rand asked, forcing flatness into his voice. He knew he was being baited. "What is amusing, doctor?"

"Nothing. Oh, nothing. Some members come in here and they think we are going to enact some ridiculousness like from The Manchurian Candidate. We don't have time for mindless drones, for half-zombies fried out of their heads on LSD or subliminal mind control. We want thinkers. Just thinkers, though. Thinkers who can, as I said yesterday, separate their passion from their reason."

Rand nodded.

"For once, I did not know what I was expecting from you today," Virgillius said, now giving his full gaze to Rand. "Were you going to be anxious today? Cocky? Proud of your actions yesterday? Regretful? Your answer earlier was good, but let's try again. How are you today, Rand?"

"Haven't we already gone through this?"

"Bear with me, Rand."

"I feel okay."

"Come on, Rand. So much progress earlier, so much description and now, 'okay'? What a lackadaisical response. Am I talking to a fourth grader now? You're much, much better than that, I – "

"Fine," Rand cut him off, measuring his words carefully. "I am slightly fatigued mentally and physically. The last few days have been an adrenaline filled ride. I am slightly apprehensive, mainly because I do not care for that," he motioned to the mirror. "Or that."

He pointed to the movie screen.

Virgillius studied him.

"And why is that, Rand? What do you fear behind the mirror?"

"I fear nothing behind the mirror. I just prefer to see who I am performing for," he said.

"Performing? Is this all a performance?"

Damn. Rand thought, another slippage.

"Performing is the wrong word, ah, er, incorrect description. I do not appreciate the unknown factor of who might be observing me or judging my actions thus I feel apprehensive. The unknown in this case can incite concern and caution."

"Ah," Virgillius punched in something on his tablet. "Much, much better. Your jargon is improving. Remember, there is no feeling. Only reason. I see you are learning that. Lose your feeling, lose your fear."

Rand was silent.

"So, Rand, you are now here – what, four, five days and already you've shown so much promise that Kent has placed you in our accelerated program. What do you think about that?"

"I think it is good. If I can use the word good, not in the moral sense. I should say, it is positive. It is encouraging. It holds promise and I am enjoying learning and experiencing a world previously unknown to me."

Silence.

Virgillius staring at him.

"How much do you know about your parents, Rand?"

The question momentarily shocked him, threw his senses for a loop. He blinked. Steeled himself. Sons of bitches, he told himself. That came out of left field. They really are testing me.

"Pardon me?" he stalled.

"You heard me. How much do you know about your parents?"

"I, mean, well, I know tons about them. They were...my parents. I know them as my mother and father. That could be expanded on forever...I don't know what you want -"

"This is good, but more. More concrete. Less how you felt about them. More about what you knew."

Rand took a deep breath.

"I know about their work, their kindness, their love for me, their passion for learning and teaching...I mean the list goes on...do you want me to give you an oral biography or a detailed psychoanalytic impact of how they raised me? Nature versus nurture? Do you want me to analyze them from a Freudian standpoint or use Jung's ideas? I can type a synopsis out if you like?"

"No, no. You can imagine we have all that here."

Right, Rand thought. So why are you asking me this question? The subject of his parents was not taboo, but close to it. Even among his closest friends, it was a subject he rarely broached. A subject, a part of his life, he had worked at skimming over, at letting the scar tissue of not only their death, but his existence with them only exist as a shadowy, buried chapter.

"What can I do for you, then?"

"I think the question," Virgillius said, "is what can we do for you?"

"Very well," the old cat and mouse game again.

"Did you know your parents were involved with us?"

Rand stiffened, felt his fists tighten involuntarily, willed them to relax. Forced his face to remain impassive.

"No, I did not. I imagined they might have been, after everything the last few days, but I wasn't sure," he lied.

"Yes, oh, yes, they spent many years working for us. Your father, in particular, had a penchant for our mission. Like your grandfather, his intellect, loyalty and curiosity combined to make him a formidable part of our family."

Rand silent.

Virgillius leaned back in his chair, assuming the look of an executive, instead of a scientist. Rand could feel Dunkel's eyes on him, too. Wondered who was behind the mirror.

"They were quite good. Most of their work was done in the late stages of The Cold War. You can imagine how challenging it must have been to secure access to areas behind the Iron Curtain. But they did it. It always draws less attention if you travel in a pair – male and female - and they made an exceptional team. Your father could switch in and out of identities in a heartbeat. His adeptness at language and cultural norms was a great trait. Your mother, well her beauty was only surpassed by the looks of innocence she used," Virgillius smirked. "It gained us great access. A matter of fact, one of our largest finds in the 70s was attributed to them. A stone unearthed in the Karalveem Valley in the USSR in what was initially a mining operation opened many doors for us. They went in, secured the area, paid off the local officials, employed massive misinformation with the military operations in the region and then successfully had the stone removed and taken to one of our locations."

Rand sat. Quiet. How was he to respond? Surprised? Impressed? Upset?

Virgillius studied him. The only sound was their breathing.

"Questions so far?"

"No, just finding this very interesting." Rand felt like a robot spilling out a script.

A slight nod.

"This is a long story, Rand, and I am not as verbose as Kent. I am not skilled in the arts of vernacular," a barely perceptible nod to the mirror, "so let me cut to the bone of the matter. Your parents were good people. They were exceptional academics, diligent workers, possessed great instincts and were well aware of the world around them. They were, for the most part, an integral part of The Organization…. but then, they faltered. They waded into waters of moral ambiguity. They began to question our motives, our directives and so forth. I imagine part of the impetus for their change of thinking was your birth. Raising a child and all the psychological changes one undergoes during that period can often lead to odd revelations or changes of course in one's own life. People begin to use words like, 'ethics' and 'character' and 'the right thing to do.' Soon, their questions became more than an annoyance, but a challenge. Sometimes very directly, especially your father. At some point, they decided to take action. They threatened us. They wanted to expose our mission. Of course, that was unacceptable. That was when they were killed."

Virgillius stared at him. A hard stare. Again, Rand felt like a specimen.

"Questions, Rand?"

Confusion, fury, rage, more confusion. Above all, shock. He willed it shut. Barely. Tried to keep his voice from quivering. Bile rising in his throat. The shock helped. He felt detached. Like he was watching himself perform. Listening to himself talk. Saw himself from above. Like in a play or a dream.

"Killed? Doctor, I think you are mistaken. They were in a car crash. It was on New Year's Eve, coming home from a party. Icy roads, a drunk driver. Almost a fucking cliché way to go, but they died in an accident. A car accident."

"Oh yes, a car accident. Right, Rand. A car accident where both your parents were killed. And your parents' car caught fire and exploded before the police could arrive at the scene. And the driver of the other car said he remembered nothing of the night which would make sense since his blood alcohol level was way above the legal limit. The rest of the toxicology report went missing. And then he died in jail before the trial. What was his name? James Guthrie, a philandering chef, right? No witnesses. Very little evidence of what actually happened. All sewn up tightly. Only one piece left to the puzzle: Ten-year-old Rand O' Neal. Yes, you, Rand. You were the only part of the equation unharmed. Staying safe with your grandparents that night. Do you remember? Actually how could you forget, I imagine. Safe and cozy at your grandparents' home, probably sitting with your grandfather by the fire. Your grandfather who had agreed to their demise only on the condition of sparing you. Do you remember him that night, Rand? Think hard. You were young and have probably blocked it out – typical coping mechanism – but, think, do you remember? He was drunk. Beyond New Year's Eve drunk, wasn't he? I believe – "

"Enough!" Rand shouted. "Enough God damn you! Enough! You're lying!" The words exploded and Rand found himself on his feet. Hands gripping the side of the table, towering over Virgillius who, stared back at him with his reptilian eyes.

"Am I Rand? What do you think? This is a test? No, we aren't complete sadists. This is the truth. But if you are to continue your training, then –"

"I said enough God damn it," Rand flipped the table over, did not expect it to be so flimsy and light. It landed on Virgillius, pinning him between it and his chair.

"Help!" the scientist yelled. Dunkel moved slowly toward them.

Rand picked the table off of Virgillius. But there was no intention of help in his movements. He yanked him to his feet. His right arm was cocked and the rage flew through him, his fist getting to finally connect with the smug visage of the scientist.

Then everything went black.

CHAPTER SIXTY-ONE

Evening again. Or was it dawn? Rand could not tell anymore. He was back in his room. Face away from the windows. Watching the almost familiar patterns of shadow and light play on the wall. A breeze on his skin, goose bumps rising.

He rolled over. The tired deep yellow on the mountains looked like dusk. He sat up. Felt a pain in his back. Reached around. A Band-Aid. Ripped it from the skin. Rubbed his finger underneath. No abrasion, just a slight swelling. Ah, Rand thought, a needle. A damn hypodermic syringe filled with God-knows-what. Thought about the smiling face of Dunkel. The smirk on Virgillius's face. The words about his parents. His parents. Part of The Organization? Killed? With his grandfather knowing? A revelation? True? No. Maybe? Couldn't handle it right now. Shoved it back inside of him. Another day. He couldn't deal with it now. Had to compartmentalize.

At least he had rested well. Dreamless. How long had he been out? A night? A day? Two days? This damn place was making him crazy. Days and nights bled together. Too much. Too much of everything. Living two lives. Thinking one thing. Telling them another. He was determined to play the role to get in The Organization. To get in to destroy it. He had to. But, while it was easy to bullshit one's way through a cocktail party or an interview, keeping the mask on under this duress was nearly impossible. He felt himself breaking. He knew a divergence was coming. An impasse loomed. His pants lay folded on the chair. He reached in the pocket, withdrew the pack of cigarettes and began to smoke. Finished his cigarette. Lit another. Then another.

CHAPTER SIXTY-TWO

The knock had come at the door. This time there was the forgetful faced servant. The coffee. A note on the tray invited him to dinner with Kent. There was no time on it. Rand gave a wry smile. Of course, there couldn't be a time, he didn't have a clock in his room. He dressed. Was waiting on the elevator to open when Hope came walking down the hall.

He gave a half-wave. She smiled back.

"Hey, lady," he called out awkwardly. "I haven't seen you in a couple of days."

Words fumbling. Remembering their last meeting.

He could see her forcing a smile.

"It has been a while."

Rand stared at her, sides of his mouth crinkling, licked his lips.

She cocked her head. "How are you?"

"Just…weird, I don't know…I'm lost…I'm tired, Hope." His honesty surprised him and apparently her as well.

"What's going on Rand?"

"I have no clue."

"That might be the most honest thing you've said since I met you. Are you undergoing some type of experiments or something? I heard they do that to some of the new recruits who are late bloomers as they say. I never went through it, thank God, but, you look terrible."

"Thanks sweetheart." He tried to control the acidity in his tone.

"Seriously, you need some fresh air."

"I need more than that."

"Where are you going?"

He just raised his eyebrows and nodded his head.

"Again?" she whispered. "Be careful, Rand. You may think you're a fair-haired child. You may even be one. But you may just be a plaything too. An experiment. Kent is, well…a sadist in many ways…Don't be fooled by his smooth words. He is more devilish than he is clinical…I don't know…just be careful…"

"I'm trying."

The elevator door whisked open. Rand felt a body pass them in the hall. Did not look to see who it was.

"Well, for whom the bell tolls." He said, offered a half grin.

"Come by later if you can," she lightly touched his hand.

CHAPTER SIXTY-THREE

"Another exciting morning with the doctor?" Kent stood facing the window, cigarette in hand, smoke lazily curling upwards.

Rand wondered if he was always like this. He had never seen the man touch a computer, dictate a letter and, only on occasion, with a phone. Was he always thinking? Was he always at the window? Or was it simply a power move he used for Rand's benefit?

"Yes sir," Rand answered, trying to keep the edge out of his voice. "Very enlightening."

Kent turned, a slight wince to his smile.

"I'm sorry for the sedative, but you left us with little choice. More than the sedative, though, I'm sorry you had to hear the truth about your parents in that setting, but I hope you know why it was necessary. We need everything from you – your trust, your understanding, your complete loyalty - if we are to move forward."

Rand was silent. Directed his eyes again to the painting above Kent's fireplace.

"I completely understand you attacking Dr. Virgillius, Rand, I do. But, unfortunately, that rage set you back in not only his eyes, but mine as well."

Rand waited. Waited for the condescending words. The lecture.

"I want you to continue with Virgillius in a few days. I still think you have a future here, but I am hoping a night in The Lab might enlighten you and aid you in understanding us more. Understanding the importance, the gravity of what we do, the reason we require such devotion. Such, sometimes, blind devotion. Complete loyalty. I think an hour in The Lab can usher you along."

"The Lab?"

"Yes, The Lab. That is what we call it. Did I not tell you? It is in a chamber within The Cavern. It is where we house the stones."

"Okay."

"Good. You still have your visitor's pass, I see. Go down there after dinner. You probably need some food on your stomach and more coffee to give you a clear head. I'll have Dr. Lightfoot waiting for you. You two seem to have formed a connection….If my schedule permits, I will join you both later. "

Kent turned back to the window, extinguishing his cigarette in one of his upright ash trays. Stood rigid, then turning to Rand.

"Well, what are you waiting for?"

"I thought dinner was here?"

"No, a flimsy excuse to talk to you. Go to the cafeteria if you wish. But don't be long. I am calling Dr. Lightfoot shortly and you need to get to work."

CHAPTER SIXTY-FOUR

The badge still scanned in as valid, but as he waited to be admitted to The Cavern, tiny beads of sweat broke out on his forehead.

"You still aren't cleared for thumbprint scans, but Mr. St. James called down and said you were good to go. He overrode the system with a rarely-used executive code. Dr. Lightfoot is waiting inside."

Rand heard the lock to the tall door click open and he walked in. The door closing behind him, he wiped his brow and took a deep breath.

Her saw her, waiting for him in The Cavern's eerie half-light. Standing.

"Let's go. Follow me," she said. No returning glance. No flirtation. Pure business. Damn, Rand thought. The last thing I need is confusion from a woman in the midst of all this.

They wound through the room, past the countless shelves stacked with scrolls, past the darkened room where the Atlantean stones stood and other darkened cases that held God knows what other treasures.

Eventually the room narrowed and they came to a stainless steel door, oddly out-of-place among the Old Word antiquities, the mysterious dim rooms and ancient books.

Hope approached the door and pressed a green button sunk into the wood beside it. The door slid open and Rand followed. Gone was the inviting light of banker's lamps and the plush leather chairs. Instead the chamber reminded Rand of the antiseptic offices plucked from Virgillius's haunts. The walls and the floor a harsh white with the same plastic-like veneer on their surface.

To his right, Rand spied a conference room, sealed off by glass on all sides, a quartet of scientists sat amidst a conglomeration of computers and monitors. In swiveled chairs, they shuttled across the floor, punching in data, staring at the monitors. Apparent silence between them. No acknowledgement paid to Rand and Hope.

And, there, in the center of the chamber itself, encased in what appeared to be a type of glass was what Rand instinctively knew was the stone itself.

The latest piece of the Slendoc Meridian he had helped extract from the mountainside just a couple of days ago.

Rand detected a faint hum. The air seemed somewhat electrified. Nothing dangerous, just the strange, hairs-on-the-neck feeling one gets before a thunderstorm strikes or walking through the woods alone at night.

When Hope spoke, Rand felt himself jump.

"This is it," she said.

Rand tried to agree.

"Yeah, I mean. Here it is…I saw it a few days ago when we pulled it from the earth, remember?"

"You saw part of it a few days ago, but only the crown. But this is it. This is the stone itself. Unearthed. The grime cleaned away, the dirt washed off. Now. Beautiful. In all its brilliance."

"For it being so powerful, it sure seems to be protected pretty flimsily. What is that, glass?"

"It's a tempered glass, just a few inches thick. Not as tough as bulletproof glass, but stronger than it looks. Its strength is not the glass itself, but chemicals embedded in it that keep the energy, the dominance of the stone at bay. As with many things, what you see is not exactly what you get. Illusion. Could you break that glass with say, repeated blows or gunshots? Yes. But it is not the physical properties that give it its protection to us, it is the chemical properties. Like those suits we wore when we dug it up. They weren't thick, but they were resilient, specifically configured with electro-magnetic sensors and embedded with certain chemical compounds to ward off the effects of the stone. Make sense?"

"Yes. Very much so."

"Good."

"Any other questions?"

"I can't help but ask. This room is hundreds of feet underground, we have to go past a guard station to get here, use a thumbprint scanner, and then, this room here, the entire point of this operation, I guess, is not even guarded? This seems a little ridiculous."

"That is the intention. Enough grandeur. We wanted this section of the operation to be purely pragmatic. And if something changes, or something develops, or God help us we have an emergency, the last thing we need are a dozen scientists trying to get their handprints or retina scans correct when we might have a crisis on our hands in there. We need a quick and simple exit and entrance. And you have to realize, if they've made it this far, we have really little to fear in regards to security."

"Makes sense."

No reply.

"Any more questions?"

Good God, Rand thought, she sounds like a tour guide.

"No, ma'am."

"Very good. You want to see the other stones, I imagine, other pieces we've found through the years. They are farther back. Follow me."

They gingerly walked around the stone, Rand entranced by its shifting blues and silvers, wanting to stop, but Hope grabbed his arm and ushered him down another hall and into another chamber. Rand had to squint into the half-darkness. But, as she led him forward the light began to shift. Gradually, a flicker of blue here, a cobalt hue there. Then, as they walked on, the light began to increase. And increase. Odd shadows and lights danced on the floor. Blues, silvers darting in and out. The light emanated from several, maybe dozens, of stones scattered throughout the room. All enclosed in the same type of glass. Different sizes, different heights, different widths. Some shards. Some perfectly round, some oblong. All of them throwing off color.

The main room. The holy land. Ground zero.

The strange, electrification was more present. He felt slightly nervous, anxious, yet, he had little fear. The feeling of electricity as he had described it to Kent was here. Not quite as powerful as when he was in the earth with The Bear, but he could sense a change in the atmosphere.

Rand followed Hope to the middle of the room.

"Damn," he whispered to himself. "This is amazing. I had no idea there were this many pieces."

"There is always more than you know, Rand. You should have figured that out by now."

"I guess so."

Then suddenly, Hope turned, grabbed his shoulders.

"Rand, you need to get out of here. As soon as you can."

Rand backed away, easing her hands off his shoulders.

"Easy. Whoa. Why are you telling me this now? You've been distant as hell all morning, acting all know-it-all snob scientist and now you're giving me a warning? Where the hell did this come from? Come on, why am I supposed to believe you now – "

"Don't be so obtuse. Do you see any video cameras in here?"

Rand looked around. In the corners. At the ceiling, the walls. There was nothing remotely like a video camera or anything electrical at all. No outlets. No computers. Not even a light switch.

"No."

"Exactly. That is why I had to wait."

"Had to wait? For what? Is this a set up? Why wouldn't there be security cameras in here? I mean this room is probably the most valuable of all isn't it?"

"Yes, it is. But the energy from these stones – even encased – fries every circuit we attempt to put in here. Audio and visual. We can't even install your average 40 watt bulb in here from all the power of these stones together. Ironically, the only safe place to talk in this whole complex is the most protected area."

Rand gave a wry smile. "That is pretty screwed up."

"Listen. No time for your jokes. Something is changing here. In The Organization. I can't put my finger on it, but things are changing. Our ideals are never mentioned anymore, our goals are never talked about, there are too many secrets. Too many circles within circles. It used to never be like that. And I overheard Kent saying something to the effect of this latest find, 'completing the cycle' and 'full-scale control.'"

"What do you mean? Control of what?"

"Control of everything. Rand, I don't know what to do. I'm scared. And I'm scared for you."

"Well, that's great. Scared for me. What the hell? You think I haven't been scared the last week or however long I've been in here? I haven't exactly been having the time of my life. Chased. Shot at. Kidnapped. Drugged. Interrogated. Yeah, great fucking times. I can't tell you the last time I had so much fun," the sarcasm flowed freely now. "And, oh yeah, there is the gorgeous woman I met who I spent a great night with. The problem is, I don't know her. Or maybe I do know and kind of like her. Smart.

Intelligent. A wit. Damn beautiful. But, who knows. What if she is playing me, lying to me, setting me up? Nothing like a sense of paranoia with some chaos to give somebody a great day. Oh yeah, very good times, actually – "

"Enough, Rand. Enough. Don't you understand? You need to get out of here."

Rand loosed a bitter laugh.

"I heard you twice the first time. Yeah, sure. Let me get out of here. Sounds great. Who do I talk to about that? Should I have Kent book me a flight to Beijing? Maybe ask him to deposit a few thousand euros into my bank account to help me get settled? Maybe Virgillius? He would be glad to see me go. I imagine he has a sporty two-seater I could use to zip through the Alps. Maybe I just walk out the front door if this place even has one."

"No, but – "

"I don't need buts. I've been looking at ways to get out of here since I woke up in this hellhole and can't find any. That is why I've been trying to get inside, so I can get outside. Don't you get it? I need to become part of The Organization to leave it. This place is on lockdown. Cameras. Heavy security. I'm locked inside my room. I'm basically dead back in Atlanta. I don't know what to do. That's why I have been playing every card I have to survive. I can't even begin to tell you the things I've had to do the past few days just to keep my head above water."

"Rand, I can understand," she said.

"Bullshit." Rand retorted, his voice just below a yell.

"Listen," she implored, grabbing him again. "There are things I saw when I came here that I fell in love with. The research, the noble intentions, the avarice of knowing the unknown, but things are spiraling too fast. I hear rumors. Information is being hidden. Several members of the scientific staff have disappeared in the last few days. I don't even know if I will survive, but, right now, it is your life that worries me. You need to go before something worse happens to you than death. Kent's using you as a plaything, an experiment or something. Time is running out. I know this for a fact. Someone told me inside his circle. You need to get out of here."

Rand shook his head.

"Okay, let's say I believe you. So what's next? Seriously, if you are being honest. What's next? I need your help, your advice. No sarcasm intended. Please, just tell me, I -"

"Please tell me what?" the voice came from behind them. The accent easy to recognize now. The gait straight and purposeful. The suit unmistakable and the face, even in the shifting lights, recognizable. It was Kent.

How long had he been there? How much had he heard? Neither one of them had heard his footsteps. Rand reacted quickly.

"Ah, Kent, thank goodness, Dr. Lightfoot thinks she can't tell me about all the stones because of my relative newness here, but I am very interested. She won't budge, even with the magic word 'please'," he gave an artificial grin. "How about it now? With you here, perhaps you can convince her, or even better yourself, illuminate me."

Kent gave them both an appraising look before the familiar smugness returned.

"How much have you told him, Hope?"

"Very little. Very little. I was just giving him the dime tour," if she was caught off guard she didn't show it. "Just letting him have a peek of our stones in their collective glory. Was debating on telling him more later. But, right now, just showing a glimpse of our hand is the way I believe you put it."

Kent smiled.

"Yes, that is the way I put it. Just a little bit at a time. Well, Rand? Initial thoughts?"

"Very impressive. I thought The Cavern was impressive, but this is beyond what I expected. So many stones…"

The reptilian smile.

"Good. Good. Just a taste for you. I didn't think I could make it for your tour down here, but my meeting got postponed. Regardless, it looks like I missed the best part of it. I always enjoy the look on the faces when I reveal our stones. Ah, just to capture it for a minute. The pure awe. It is divine. Helps keep one going when things get tough. Let's let this settle in and then we can answer those questions you had for Dr. Lightfoot tomorrow. It is getting rather late."

CHAPTER SIXTY-FIVE

Tomorrow.

Tomorrow couldn't come soon enough for Rand. He was alert. On edge. Back in his room, sitting on his bed, the windows open. Not even a thought of sleep after the words that Hope had told him. After seeing the chamber of stones.

There was no clock in his room, but he knew it was sometime around 1 a.m. There had been no invitation to Kent's quarters after their visit to The Cavern. Rand had gone back to the cafeteria and eaten alone, stabbing his rubbery meat with a plastic fork, moving soggy vegetables on his plate and sipping from a bottled water.

He had stopped by Hope's room on the way back to his room. Knocked. Waited. Knocked again. No answer. Wondered where she was. He was still at an impasse with his thoughts on her. Was she for real? Was she on his side? Was she playing him? Was she meeting with Kent right now? Maybe planning out a neat-nicked execution for him?

He had consciously shoved the thoughts out of his mind then. Had to focus. Could not worry.

He did the same now. Stared out the window. Forced his panic down. Went to pick up the pack of cigarettes. Stopped. Waited. Thought he heard something in the hall. But, it didn't matter. He was locked in from the outside. A sardonic smile on his face. How serious everything was and yet how ludicrous at the same time. He gingerly emptied a cigarette from the pack, the flick of the lighter crackling across the room. He inhaled, held it, pushed the blue smoke from his lungs out the window and watched it dissipate into the sky, knowing that any other time, any other circumstance and this would be the perfect vacation. The mountains in the distance, the snow on their peaks shimmering faintly under a full moon. The scents from the garden below and the fertile earth smells from fields beyond.

He started to take a second drag, lifting the cigarette to his lips. A noise in the hall again.

"Damn it," he muttered. Stubbed his cigarette out on the window sill. Crept to the door, leaning against the wall behind it. If anyone was going to come in, they would be in for a surprise. He debated on tossing pillows in his bed and covering them up to construct a make-shift false body under the sheets, but he was too tense. Too ready. Did not want to lose any advantage of surprise with his back to the door.

The knob jittered. Stopped. Twitched again. It seemed like someone was picking the lock. What the hell? Then he heard the bolts slide back. The knob turned all the way. An arm entered, reached upward for the light switch. Rand grabbed it by the wrist, yanked the body into the room, fist raised to pummel the intruder. Whoever it was, was caught off guard, a body unbraced and surprisingly light. He heard a wince. Stumbling. Slammed the door closed behind him with his foot. His nerves erupted into an adrenaline rush. Fists up, advancing on the form that had fallen onto the floor. He would not go down without a fight.

"You stupid, stupid man!"

"What?" the voice shocked him. A female.

"Stupid man. God, you're daft. You hurt my arm you brat."

He recognized the voice now. Hope's voice. Irritation and anger saturating her words. Rand flipped on the light switch. She stood, brushing her clothes off. Hair disheveled. Rubbing her wrist.

"I'm sorry, I thought you were someone else."

She just glared at him.

"Is your wrist okay?"

"I'm fine. Probably just a nasty bruise. You are a tight wound wire."

"Hey, what do you expect?" A flat statement, not a question. "What are you doing here?"

She closed the space between them, wrapped her arms around his frame and pressed her lips to his. A solid kiss. Almost passionless, but firm, strong, focused.

He responded tentatively, his hormones kicking in before stopping.

"Wait a second, what's going on – "

He couldn't finish his sentence. She was pressing against him again, the lips locked firmly on his. Then the darting entrance of her tongue. He felt her breasts rubbing against his chest, nipples rubbing into his chest, her fingers running through his hair. She began pushing him toward the bathroom. He kept his eyes open. His senses aware. Listened to the door behind him. Waited for it to open. Waited for the sound of footsteps. This would be a perfect time for one of their damn syringes he thought. She pushed him, almost violently, into the bathroom. Reached around him, turned on the shower to full blast. Then stopped, stared at him.

"My, my, professor, you sure are amorous tonight," Rand said.

"Shut up. There is no time for your smart ass observations."

"Wait a damn second. You just came barging in here, lured me into the bathroom, turned on the shower. I feel like we're in a porno movie."

She moved to him. No embrace this time. Just brought her mouth to his ear.

"You know this place is bugged and probably has cameras in it, too. I doubt they have bugs in the bathroom, but if they do, they won't be able to hear us whisper over the noise from the shower. I just need you to listen and follow my instructions."

Rand nodded slowly.

"Now, here is why I came," the whisper in his ear continued, her hands now planted firmly on his shoulders. "They're going to use you tomorrow in some type of experiment. I don't know what. Something with the new stone under the guise of your recruitment which is a sham. I know this because I was told by a friend inside their damn circle. And he wanted me to warn you. As a favor, some type of loyalty to your grandfather."

"I appreciate it, but that information is about as useful as tits on a boar hog."

"What?"

"Sorry, it's an old Southern expression. But what can I do? I'm below low man on the totem pole. Do you have any ideas?"

"I've got something arranged," a distinct nervousness in her voice now. "Listen. A helicopter is leaving in less than 10 minutes to go back near the site where we discovered the last stone. It is a routine trip to change shifts. They're still searching for any fragments of the stone in the area. Typical procedure, but never mind that. You can ride with me in the helicopter. I've already taken care that you won't be on the log. Halfway there, we're going to make a quick stop. That's when you disappear. Leave the helicopter and run. I've got a bag with some tricks in it – a suit to mask your body heat from infrared cameras, a compass, food, map and a gun. You need to make it east over the mountains, there is a railway station about - "

"Whoa, whoa, whoa," Rand said, arms rising, backing away from the embrace. "Slow down. What about you? They're going to see you with me when they review video footage. What are you going to tell them?"

She shot him a glare, pulled him back toward her, the mouth near his ear.

"Don't raise your voice, damn it. I will tell them nothing. I had no knowledge. I'll tell them the usual, how you forced me into the copter, threatened me. I will need for you to hit me – uh, you know to make a bruise somewhere. The other thing – "

"You've really thought this through, haven't you?"

"Why wouldn't I? And I've had help. What, you think I would suggest you sprint out the gate while bribing the guards with a Hershey bar?"

"Did you say the chopper is leaving in ten minutes?"

She glanced down at her watch, fanning her hand to dissipate the fog steaming up the bathroom.

"We're down to eight."

"Okay then," he took a deep breath.

"Yes. Pack whatever you need, I – "

"I don't have anything in case you forgot."

"Okay, let's go," she said moving to the bathroom door.

"Wait," he said. "How do we do this? I mean, going down the hall. If we're on a live feed and I hold you like a hostage it will be obvious and I will be dead in a heartbeat."

"Just walk by me. Hold my hand. Trust me."

CHAPTER SIXTY-SIX

T hey had forsaken the elevator and taken a flight of stairs up a few stories to the roof where the chopper was already preparing for departure. The blades whirring, slicing the air overhead. They walked toward it, the artificial wind beating their naked heads, pushing them down. Rand recognized the face in the window, the pilot from his first flight, gave a slight nod. Hope slid open the door, shouted an apology on running late. The pilot nodded his head.

She climbed in, Rand behind her in a half-crouch. Then he stopped. Stood. Stared up. The moon was almost at its zenith, flooding its luminous waves of light on the mountains. A cast of stars around her, winking in approval at the land below. His hand was damp from holding Hope's. His vision was clear. Everything slowed down. Even the whirring of the blades slicing through the air became silent. He didn't believe in visions. Or epiphanies. Such moonlight and magnolia mysteries had been banished from his head a long time ago when his parents' bodies were lifted into an ambulance. His sense of wonder crucified among the wreckage of their car.

But, now, he sensed something. Something tugged at him.

He looked at Hope. She mouthed something he could not hear. Motioned toward him. Gesturing.

He leaned toward her, his hands balancing on the door of the chopper.

"I'm not coming," he shouted.

"What?" she shouted back, now craning her neck toward him.

He pulled her face toward him, his mouth to her ear.

"I'm not coming."

Confusion washed her face. Agony almost. She froze for a minute.

"Why?"

"I have something to finish."

The confusion again, this time mixed with agony.

"They're going to kill you."

"I know. Unless I kill them first."

She stared at him. The pilot shouted something back, jabbed his thumb in the air. Time to go.

"I don't know, Rand. Are you sure?" she asked.

"Yes."

A worrisome frown on her face.

She reached back into the chopper, grabbed a backpack and handed it to him.

"You might need this."

He nodded. No words to say now. His course was set. No time for sentimental soliloquies or goodbyes. He started to turn.

"Wait," she shouted, motioned for him to come close. She pulled his head to his, whispered in his ear. "Good luck, Rand O'Neal. I wish I knew you in another life."

He pulled back. She smiled wanly, a hint of a tear in her eyes.

"Me too," He shouted and then gave her a mournful smile. He waved his hand and started to walk away. Behind him he heard the chopper lift off splicing the night air, felt the last of the wind lashings tousle his hair. Didn't look back.

CHAPTER SIXTY-SEVEN

R and's footsteps echoed through the stairwell. He was formulating a plan on the run. Reinventing. Calculating. One way now, he knew. If he had time, he could create a plan more in-depth, add more illusion, more thought, more planning. But time was up as Hope had said and he knew she was right.

He reached the floor where his room was, cracked open the door and peered out into the empty hall. Began walking toward the elevator when he found exactly what he needed. A bathroom. Empty. Found a stall. Locked it behind him. Opened the back pack. Everything was in there. Just like Hope said. He slipped on the jacket. Found the gun. A Beretta with a laser sight attached. Already loaded and ready to go. Three magazines. He slipped it into his waistband, untucked his shirt over it, jammed the magazines into the jacket's pockets. The rest of the backpack was useless. This was a no return trip, he knew. No need for rations or maps. He zipped it up, unlocked the stall and stuffed it in the trashcan. Took a deep breath, looked at himself in the mirror. "Here goes," he muttered.

He stepped out of the bathroom and bumped into Dr. Virgillius.

"Ah, excuse me," Rand said, a slight nervousness to his voice.

"Excuse me," Virgillius responded in kind. Then the keen eyes began studying him. Always those eyes, Rand thought. Rand felt himself growing nervous. Too much was at stake now. And his will to camouflage his intent was waning as he was ready for action, had tired of talking, of lying, of creating a new identity.

"What are you doing about at this hour?" the question was neither accusatory nor genuine. Another analysis for the soulless freak, Rand thought.

"Actually, I was looking for you."

"For me?"

"Yes. I was summoned to The Cavern. To the stones. We were working on an issue and they sent me to find you. Something is acting up with one of the scientists down there and the wiring is shot so we couldn't call or page you. I volunteered to come up and do it the old fashioned way by walking around. Looks like luck favors the bold."

Virgillius tilted his head.

"Who is they? Who is down there at this hour important enough to summon me? I thought we – well some of us – were meeting in Kent's study tonight."

"We were. Change of plans. You know how it goes. Some new wrinkle in the makeup of this new stone that is bringing....new behaviors. Kent wanted you especially to monitor everything objectively if you know what I mean…your insight into their behavior, their reactions right now is imperative." Again, Rand felt as if he were reading from a script the lies flowed so easily.

Virgillius found the answer appropriate.

"Of course. Of course. These ventures can take strange turns and, as you know, as much as we know about these stones each one is different."

"Oh yes."

The two walked to the elevator.

The ride below seemed to take longer than usual. Rand stared at the ceiling, the muted steel reflecting its malicious fun-house vision back at him.

"Why the devil are you wearing that strange coat?"

Rand was silent.

"Are you cold?" the eyes were back, studying him. Calculating.

"No, I was outside on the landing pad a few minutes ago. A chill sprang up."

"I thought you said you were looking for me."

"I was."

Silence. Rand quickly cut it.

"I mean, I was on the landing pad when they called me down to The Cavern. Then they sent me back up to look for you. I guess I forgot to take it off. So much excitement tonight, you know?"

The beady eyes didn't leave his. Rand could feel them bearing into his face.

The elevator stopped. Doors opened.

The two security guards.

"Good evening, gentlemen."

"Doctor."

Virgillius showed his ID. They eyed it, slid it into a scanner and held it back.

"Thank you, doctor."

Rand close behind him.

"Wait, sir. We need your card."

CHAPTER SIXTY-EIGHT

R and felt like he was at the edge of a high dive when he was a child. He wanted to jump, but he did not want to and he knew once he did, there was no stopping. Time slowed down. He waited. Stood. Silent.

"Sir, your card." the guard said again.

"Ah, sorry, here you go." Rand handed it over. A red light came up.

"You're not cleared without an executive order."

"But, I was just down here, remember? They sent me up to find him," pointing at Virgillius. "We're in a hurry."

"Yes," Virgillius interrupted, impatient. "He was just down here a few minutes ago. He's with me."

"Uh, sorry, Doctor. I haven't seen him in hours. Mr. St. James hasn't called back with an override, we need to –"

He never finished his sentence. Even if he could've no one would have heard the words from the gunshot that reverberated off the walls. Rand had whipped out the gun from his waistband and fired point blank at the guard, the first bullet whizzing over his head burying itself in the concrete behind him, the second striking him in the chest. The guard fell back. Hit the floor violently.

Rand turned quickly, saw the other guard raising his machine gun.

"Don't do that," Rand said, his gun already aimed at the man. The laser sight easily emblazoned on the man's forehead.

Rand saw hesitation in his eyes.

"Don't do it. You don't want this. I don't want this. Put your hands up."

The guard hesitated. Rand felt his patience dissolve.

"Raise your hands! Do it now!" he yelled.

He saw the guard reach for the trigger.

Rand squeezed off three shots. His hand had been shaking this time and only one bullet hit the man, but it hit where it count, splitting the man's throat in two, his head dangling on a piece of twiny flesh. Surprise still in his eyes as he fell back to the floor.

Rand looked at Virgillius who stared back at him. Frozen in mid-stride. Confusion on his face. Then his eyes flicking to behind Rand.

The first guard Rand had shot was rising to his feet. He saw now. Craters in the man's chest. Bulletproof vest.

"Damn."

Before the guard could grasp his weapon from the floor, Rand ran at him, kicked him to the ground and pistol whipped him in the head. The man crumpled and lay flat on his face, a thin stream of blood from his ear. Rand's ears ringing from the gunshots in the hall. He leaned over, pilfered the grenades from the guard's bandolier and slung the machine gun over his shoulder. Turned and saw Virgillius at the door pressing his thumb manically onto the scanner. He turned and looked at Rand. The first look of any emotion Rand had ever seen on the man's face.

Fear.

The fear only lasted a moment before panic took over. The door unlocked. Virgillius slid inside the door, closing it fast behind him. But Rand was quicker, stuck his foot in. Felt Virgillius pulling in vain on the other side. Rand stuffed the handgun into his waistband and using both his hands pried the door open. Virgillius backed away, the look of a trapped rat on his face. A mix of fear, sickening rage and simmering anger.

"What are you doing?" he demanded.

"Shut up." Rand delivered flatly, then turned and shot the handle off the door.

He leveled the gun at Virgillius.

"Come on, let's go."

"What? Go where?"

Rand motioned toward the back of The Cavern. Virgillius hesitated, then reluctantly began walking. Rand came up behind him, placed the gun at the bottom of the man's back, ushering them forward. Eyes scanning The Cavern for anyone else. Empty. Good.

Virgillius stopped. Wheeled on him.

"Wait. Wait. You need to stop this."

"Stop what?"

Rand briefly felt a slight tinge of amusement at how the tables had turned. He momentarily reveled in the cat and mouse game. This time, finally the cat. Virgillius finally relenting his logic-filled mind to emotion.

"Whatever you're doing. You killing those men. I –" he fumbled for words.

Rand restrained himself from slapping him. Felt the days of controlled rage welling in him, a tinge of sadism edging on his consciousness, but shoved it down. Again. Like a fetid bile. He knew he could not lose control now. Could not waste time on this man. On pure revenge.

"Keep walking," he said, pushing Virgillius again.

Behind them, outside the main door, a siren sounded.

Virgillius wheeled on him, an arrogant sneer on his face.

"See, you won't get away with this. There are too many of us. We know – "

Rand backhanded him with the gun. Virgillius crumpled to the ground. The Italian professor cradling his head. Blood splattered from his nose onto his white lab coat like a bastardized Jackson Pollack painting. He looked at his coat, then back at Rand. The rat eyes again. Rand aimed the gun at his chest.

"Just lay on the ground and shut up."

Virgillius stared at him. Half-dazed. Half-unsure.

The siren outside the doors waned, replaced by voices. Several voices. Arguing.

They were moving faster than Rand had anticipated.

"I knew we never should have let you live," Virgillius spat out the words with a venom. "Even for a day. Even for our experiments. I knew were a threat, but no, Kent, would not listen to me. Emotional pledges to your grandfather, too dazzled by his pet project. His research. What he wanted to do to you, I – "

"For the last time shut up!" Rand shouted now. A dam burst, a wave of emotion. "Shut the fuck up!" then louder. "Shut the fuck up! You arrogant sadistic prick. I should kill you now!"

He was about to say more when he heard the beating on the doors. They were trying to break them down. Rand stepped toward Virgillius.

"Get up."

The man staggered to his feet, cupping his nose.

Rand pushed the gun to the man's temple, watched his lips quiver. The small beads of sweat on his forehead. Then he swung his arm and backhanded him again. Felt the cartilage of the man's ear dissipate under the force of the steel.

"That's for my parents, you son of a bitch."

Rand left him on the floor, bleeding and unconscious, and walked through The Cavern toward the chamber that held the stones.

CHAPTER SIXTY-NINE

The strange star light beamed onto the ceilings and the stone itself pulsated emitting beams of blue and silver throughout the room. Rand glanced around. He saw the scientists in the sealed room. Four of them. So absorbed in their work, they didn't even lift their eyes when he walked in. The sounds of the gunshots must have been muffled by the door, Rand thought.

"Everybody out now."

Either the glass was too thick or the scientists were too engrossed to hear him.

"Out now!" he shouted.

The quartet turned and looked at him. Completely unimpressed. Rand raised the gun so they could see it, held it above his head. Fired a shot. Their expressions changed immediately. Panic washing across their faces. They began to move as one, clamoring outside their pod, scrambling toward the door to pass by Rand into The Cavern. Rand focused his eyes on the stone, determined not to look at them. No eye contact. But there was one. There always is. Rand felt a small body hovering at his side.

"Excuse me," a faint Irish accent. Rand ignored him.

"Excuse me," the voice again.

Rand turned his head. Pointed the gun at the man. Saw a shrunken old visage with blazing green eyes.

"This area is very volatile. I don't know what you're doing, but if another bullet is shot in here, it could cause great danger, great calamity. I strongly urge you – "

"Get out." Rand knew time was wasting. The longer he waited, the longer anything took, the greater chance of him failing.

"But, you really need to understand, I – "

Rand pushed the gun to the man's forehead, and used it to urge him out the door. The shock on the man's face now replaced by confusion, every step backwards a little more tentative. Rand took off his jacket and jammed it into the door to keep it open. He needed to see everything around him now.

The scientists scurried behind the bookcases. The faint blue light from the stone danced on the barrel of his Beretta.

He took a deep breath. Stepped back into the room toward the stone.

He was alone.

CHAPTER SEVENTY

Again. Almost silent. Except for the humming. The slight vibration in the air.

Rand inhaled deeply. Breathed. Closed his eyes momentarily.

Walked up to the case that held the stone. Pushed it with the palm of his hand. The surface was surprisingly flexible. It bent with the pressure of his hand. He pulled his hand away. It sprung back into place. Hope had told him the truth. It was a strange hybrid of fiberglass and chemicals. A shield, but not physically thick. He took several steps back. Raised the gun. The laser point focused on the case surrounding the stone's center. Fired. Again, the deafening noise of the gunshot. The case seemed to pulsate, almost to convulse, but there weren't any holes. No spider webbed splinters. No cracks.

"Damn it!" he said.

Raised the gun up again, leveling the laser sight on the stone. His hands surprisingly unshaking.

Fired. Fired again. Again. Again.

Then, a shattering of the shield. A sound like the shattering of a thousand plates. Fragments everywhere. Splintered and falling like an ice shower. Instinctively, Rand closed his eyes, turned his back.

And then he felt it. A more intense feeling than when he discovered the stone with The Bear, but similar. And stronger. Much stronger. A current? An electricity? A surge? He couldn't place it. Didn't want to. Had to remain focused. He turned back, lifted his gun again, took a deep breath, and fired at the stone.

The bullet hit its target.

He was flung back against the wall, feeling like he was in a wave underwater. The surge again rushing around him, then through him. He felt a tide of energy rush through his limbs. The air tense. He felt odd. Beyond odd. His muscles tight. His senses alert. His mind sharp. Beyond sharp. He could see things he had not noticed before. The tiny ridges in the tiles on the floor. The fibers of his shirt, odd shaped, like a million tree stumps weaved in a drunken pattern.

He could hear his own breathing, each bit of oxygen opening up the precious alveoli sacks, then releasing back through his trachea into the air.

The gun cold in his hand. Its metal familiar, but unnatural.

His hearing sharpened.

The men were still outside the main door to The Cavern. He could not only hear the pounding on the door, but the voices behind it. Incredibly clear.

"What was that noise?"

"Never mind that, get this door down." That was Kent.

The stone stared at him. Drawing him in. He could feel its power. Luring? A need to want it. Beyond a nicotine fit. Beyond lust, power, anger, revenge. He could see now why Virgillius insisted so strictly on separating reason and emotion. His reason was fading, his emotion was rising. A craving he could not place finding its footing in him. And, yet in the growing want, somewhere beneath the otherworldly tide, he could still sense why he had shattered the glass. He had to destroy it. He had to do something to keep it from the clutches of The Organization. To cripple this group that for hundreds of years had been hidden. It was not right. But, maybe, he could embrace it? He could use the power emanating for his own. For good? He thought of Weston's words in the forest, 'Ich habe die Macht.' 'Ich habe die

Macht' Like some bastardized version of greed, the very thought of the words sickened him and he felt twisted. Torn. Now it was his. If he wanted it.

The banging on the door was growing louder. The voices.

"Do I look like I give a shit? Use the Gelignite. Blow the damn door open. I don't care about collateral damage. Do it!"

Rand could hear the guards fumbling with the charge. The scraping of soles on the floor.

"Okay, sir. Step back behind the corner. We can cover ourselves with this blast blanket. We've got about one minute to detonation."

"One minute? One fucking minute!"

"Sorry sir. We don't generally deal with explosives and haven't upgraded our – "

"Just shut up. Give me your gun. I'm going in with you."

Rand listened to them. Mesmerized by his new senses. Could almost see the bodies behind the door, like a play described on the radio. Then, in front of him, was the stone shifting light and shadows on the wall. Azure to cobalt to silver to topaz. The light was brilliant, luminous, but he did not have to shield his eyes anymore.

'Ich habe die Macht'

CHAPTER SEVENTY-ONE

R and was not surprised when he heard the door blow open. He had heard the guards counting down. He knew it was coming. He felt no shock at all. Felt strangely empowered. Calm. He stared across the expanse of The Cavern. Saw a gap where the great oaken door had once stood guard. Smoke billowing toward him. Acrid. Saw shapes in the smoke. The gun in his hand was surprisingly light. He lifted it. Fired at single shot. Heard a grunt. A body fall onto the floor. He could see amazingly well now. Could see the outlines of the faces now as the bodies clamored through the opening. Lifted the gun again. Fired. Heard a scream. Fired again. A shout.

Again. Again. A grunt. Another fall on the floor. That should keep them cautious and at bay.

He turned back toward The Lab. Eyed the stone again. What to do? What to do?

He aimed the gun at the stone and pulled the trigger. Could see the bullet barreling toward it, see it spiraling, the air itself bending into a tunnel as the bullet plunged through the air. Then. Impact. Rand watched the bullet pierce the stone. Another blinding wave hit him. And he was sitting down again. Thrown out of the room onto his back. Half-blinded, but no pain this time. He steadied himself onto one knee. Lifted the gun again. Aimed at the same place he had struck before. Pulled the trigger. Could see the bullet again, spiraling in slow motion. Watched the stone crack, tiny explosions inside the rock like fragments from firecrackers, but blue and white. Another wave swept across him, the raw energy swimming in his limbs and the stone split, its bulk crumbling in two like an apple from a cleaver.

And then the voice calling across The Cavern from behind the door. He heard the voice.

"Rand. Rand." Calm, always calm. Almost soothing, but Rand could tell something was off this time. Could detect the nervousness beneath the veneer. Kent was nervous. "Rand. Stop. Listen. Please. We can fix this."

Rand stood up, looked back into The Cavern. The smoke rising to the ceiling. Saw no shapes. Nothing, but squeezed off another round anyway. Enjoyed the sparks of the bullet as it smashed into a bookshelf, papers flung into the air, the sound of splintering wood. He found himself grinning, straying danger-ously close to a delightful sensory madness.

Silence in The Cavern.

He looked back into The Lab. It was growing warm. And the colors. The blues from the stone had deepened, their hues radiating more violently, quickly. And he heard it. A distinct hum now. Slowly growing louder.

The voice cut through the mesmorization.

"Rand, I'm coming through. Do not shoot, please. We need to talk. I have something for you. To tell you. I have not told you all. There is one more thing. One more thing your grandfather wanted you to know."

Rand levelled the gun at the remnants of the door, watched Kent step through, his soft soled shoes careful not to step on the bodies and blood strewn across the floor.

"Hands on your head," Rand said evenly.

"Rand, please," Kent said, his arms spread evenly out, the welcoming act now a hated cliché.

Rand squeezed off another shot, this one whizzing just by Kent's head and smashing into a bookcase behind him, pages and paper bursting in tiny explosions.

"Above your head, Kent. Now."

"If you wish."

Kent walked through, hands above his head, exposing his now half-drenched shirt. A smile forced on his face.

"Please, let's talk. Before you destroy one of the greatest discoveries of this generation. You are on the verge of sending us back. All back. We have come so far. This could be the final piece. You know, your grandfather said –"

"Enough about my grandfather."

"But, Rand. Listen," he said and he kept walking toward Rand. Slowly, but deliberately, with a felinic grace.

"I said enough! This isn't right. These stones, you, this whole place. I'm going to blow it all to hell and you with it."

The sadistic smile.

"You know you couldn't do that. There is too much at stake here. Too much knowledge. You have learned to love it. You wouldn't want to destroy it. To send us back to The Dark Ages. Too much here."

Kent within a few feet now.

"That's close enough." Rand said, and levelled the gun at Kent's forehead. "How do you want it Kent? Do you want to see it happen or should I kill you beforehand. Perhaps a nice knee capping would do? Yes, I could do it the old IRA way. Cripple you, then make you watch the destruction of your fucked up world."

The smile again, but with a frown on the edges of the mouth.

"You know you can't do it."

Rand heard new sounds outside the door now. His hearing hyper alert. The scraping of more boots. The breathing of the guards. The words 'tear gas' and 'plastic bullets.'

"You in the hall," Rand yelled "Toss in your guns and your explosives and I won't kill this son of a bitch. And don't even think of the tear gas. I've got a gas mask. Before you can even shoot it in here, I will blow his brains out. Don't tempt me. Toss it all in and get the fuck back in the elevator."

"Do what he says," Kent shouted over his shoulders. "Do what he says. I will be fine. Leave us."

Rand heard scuffling. More whispers. A voice from behind the door.

"Sir – "

"A gas mask? Nice bluff," Kent whispered, then raising his voice. "Do what he says and do it now."

Three guns were tossed inside the room and a bandolier of grenades and tear gas was laid inside the gap. Then he heard the shuffling footsteps. Retreating. The elevator doors. Then silence.

"We're alone, Rand."

"Yes."

"And I can see it's working on you," Kent inhaled deeply, his nostrils flaring like some deranged beast centering on a kill. "Ah, just being in the vicinity of it is working on me too. Don't you love the power of it? I can tell already how your senses have been heightened. It is glorious, isn't it? Few can handle it, but you do quite well. Of course I am not surprised, your grandfather handled it well, too. You are so much like him. Ah, the power of it. Can you feel what your true potential is? This. This – what you're feeling now – is why we guard it so closely, this is what I have been trying to get through your thick head, this – "

"Enough. Shut up you God damn devil. So fucking smooth. So convincing. But it all ends here now. This is it, Kent. This is how it ends. Do you understand? The charade is up."

"The charade is up," Kent laughed as his arms dropped to his sides. "The charade is up? The world is the charade. Have you learned nothing? Have you learned nothing? You fool. Nothing can stop us. We are beyond all. We are above, underneath, inside everything. You? You? You little piss ant of a man think you can stop this machine? This dragon? This engine that has been running for centuries?"

He laughed again. A hard laugh. Condescending.

Rage flooded Rand. He lowered his arm and squeezed the trigger. Concentration filled his every sense. The bullet precise. Sliced through Kent's kneecap. Rand saw the fragments of bone and tissue shatter, the splashes of blood flung across the floor, watched the man drop. Heard his yell. Guttural. Rage filled.

"I told you to shut the fuck up, didn't I?" Rand asked.

Kent writhed in pain. No words. Just grunts.

Rand walked by him, delivered a swift kick to his ribs. Loathed himself for the action. But felt powerful. Invincible. Kent was right. The effects of the stone were powerful. Like a drug. He had never taken cocaine. Never wanted to dance with the dark gods, but he could imagine how they felt now. He could revel in it, he knew. Could already feel his mind working at levels, speeds unknown before. Could sense things as they happened, see them slowed down, but in real time. Yet he knew he must stop it. Unlatch himself. But he knew Kent was right. There was power. Rand was torn.

"You must do the right thing," he said quietly, hoping that voicing his thoughts would make them more real. Easier to comprehend. Easier to do the right thing.

He walked over and grabbed the bandolier of grenades by what was left of the door. He counted.

Six, seven, eight. Maybe not enough to destroy anything, but a start. He had no idea how the stone
would react to the blast, but he wasn't going down
without a fight. He had come this far. Had betrayed
and been betrayed. Had killed and might be killed.

A blazing pain tore through his shoulder and
knocked him forward, the gun dropping out of his
hand, clattering to the floor. He coughed. He had
been shot. Shot. Shot. The word echoed in his mind.
Another gunshot. The wall above him dented. The
bullet missed. He knelt on the ground and looked
back. There he could see, the wriggling body of
Kent, half-standing, the knee dangling behind him,
drug along, barely kept together by a tattered stitch-
ing of tendons and skin.

Rand could see it all, could smell the blood and
the gun smoke. The smell of burnt skin in the air.
The taste of iron on his tongue. Blood. Kent, pale
and limping, lifted his gun. Fired again.

More pages exploded from the books above
Rand's head. Kent had barely missed. Rand could
see his own gun only a few feet away, began to crawl
toward it.

"No!" Kent said and fired another round, this
one narrowly missing Rand's outstretched hand.

Rand looked around. For anything. One of the
machine guns. The grenades. They were all out of
reach. He crawled toward the gun again, then broke

into a half run. The bullet knocked him down. It had hit his thigh, passed through neatly, no bones broken, Rand could tell. But he felt its burning, began to feel his strength dissipate. Felt nauseous. The loss of blood. The power of the stone. Everything colliding. Too much. His senses strong. His senses reeling. His body weak. He rolled over to see Kent lift the gun again.

"Goodbye, Rand. So much waste. So much wasted potential," he shrugged his head. "Fool."

Rand heard the gunshot. Did not feel the impact, but saw Kent's eyes bulge with surprise. A patch of red on his chest. His body fall forward. Heard it sickly hit the floor, the sound of flaccid flesh impacting the wood.

CHAPTER SEVENTY-TWO

The elevator shook. Lights blinking off and on. Somewhere below he heard the sound of explosions, like far away thunder. Hope held him closer, staunching the bleeding from his shoulder with a scarf.

"This is the end," Rand said and then in a haze of absurdity and gallows humor, he quoted Jim Morrison, "My only friend, The End. This is the end..." the half singsong. The half singsong. A soft laugh. He was fading. Hope leaned him against the cool side of the elevator.

He heard an incessant ringing of an alarm. He was fading.

"Hang on Rand. Just hang on. A little while longer," she pleaded.

The elevator lurched. Another explosion from below.

"I guess we did it," he said.

"We did it alright…I hope we did the right thing."

"We did…This is the end." The half sing song. He was fading. He remembered the explosives stacked against the stone. Hope tossing in grenade after grenade and their mad rush to the elevator door they had kept jammed open with the slouched body of Kent. He remembered crawling over it to get away. The first explosion filled the entire shaft with white light. Rand was momentarily blinded. Then there were more. Louder. Then quieter. Then louder. Now far off. Muffled. Distant. What had they wrought? He shivered.

"Hang on. Hang on." Hope again. He was leaning against her. Her soft perfume.

Fading. Fading.

CHAPTER
SEVENTY-THREE

They called it a meteor strike. Whoever they were Rand still did not know, but the newspaper in front of him bore the headlines simply.

"Rogue meteorite hits Austria: Destroys town, historic castle, hundreds feared dead."

He read the headline. Re-read it again. Started to read the article then put it down. It was too much.

On the television mounted across from his bed, he flipped through the news networks, each one describing the same scene.

CNN, BBC and Fox News had descended on the area and were interviewing residents who talked about the glowing comet they saw soaring through the sky.

Soon a shaky video emerged from a phone taken by a tourist in the area. A meteorite was clearly visible. More videos surfaced. Dozens on YouTube. Twitter feeds. All the same story. More eyewitnesses.

"How? How?" his parched voice surprising him.

"Remember everything Kent told you." Her voice was soothing, but her words unnerved him.

"What do you mean? This information is coming from them? But I thought they were destroyed. I thought we put an end to this."

"Maimed, but not destroyed. Remember what Kent told you. That wasn't their only outpost. Their only operation. That was just the oldest. The main center. The European post. There are more. On every continent. And they never relent."

THE APPENDICES

Compiled by Thomas J. Callahan

While we may not know the author's intent in this book, the allusions, philology and symbology is too great to ignore. Thus, I have taken the time to examine some of the meaning and intent behind certain names and places. To delve deeper, visit www.alexandriarising.com

William Shakespeare: The greatest playwright and poet of his time, and perhaps all time. His sayings, words and phrases are commonplace today. However, as is alluded to in this book, there were the 'lost years' when he did disappear only to emerge as a vortex of literature. The simple tremendous quality and quantity of his work has often led some scholars to believe that Shakespeare was several people as one person could not possibly produce so much in such a short period. It is a myth The Organization has fostered.

Rand: The name was mistakenly thought to be a nickname for Randolph by many. In fact, the name, "Rand" is ancient Anglo-Saxon for 'wolf shield.'

(Dr.) Henry O'Neal: Publicly known as an expert in Modern Anglo-Irish relations, one-time ambassador to Ireland, cultural diplomat and philanthropist. Though he was a professor at Emory University, O'Neal occasionally lectured Yale, Harvard and Trinity College in Dublin. He turned down numerous opportunities to further his academic career due to what he professed was a deep love of his hometown, Atlanta, from where he and his wife were both born. He was a first generation college man who graduated with multiple degrees from Harvard.

Smyrna, Georgia: A city northwest of Atlanta.

The Atlanta Observer: One of metro Atlanta's mid-sized newspapers, it focuses on covering the city's northwest suburbs. It was established in 1910 and has a reputation for bulldog journalism.

Mark Venator: Venator is Latin for 'Hunter' and Mark is named after 'Mars,' the god of war. Venator was sent to hunt Rand in this instance and as Eric mentions later is one of The Organization's overseas operatives.

Aeolus Industries: The company which Venator says he works for and is printed on his business card. In Greek mythology, 'Aeolus' was the ruler of the winds and many times referred to in the arts as one of the chief muses. He is also referenced in 'The Odyssey.'

'The Falcon cannot hear the Falconer': Rand recites this phrase in the library regarding the W.B. Yeats poem, "The Second Coming." The entire poem points to a breakdown with lines such as, "Things fall apart; the centre cannot hold;" and "blood-stemmed tide is loosed upon the world." That poem contains many allusions to world-shifting events and, according to some critics, direct relations to the Apocalypse. In many ways, Rand's off-hand jocularity precedes his events in The Cavern where things do indeed fall apart.

The O'Neal family motto: 'verum in aeternum' which translated from Latin means, 'Forever True.' It is unclear how this motto became associated with the O'Neal family. With their roots heavy in northern Ireland, the claiming of a Latin motto is atypical. This is a mystery among the O'Neals of which Rand never questions his grandfather. Some inquiries state that Henry O'Neal's father, Patrick, created the motto in an effort to distance himself from warring parties in northern Ireland to create a new slate for his family in the United States when he arrived in early 1917.

Train 42: Rand takes the MARTA Train 42 to the airport to escape his pursuers. The number, '42' is widespread in the works of author Lewis Carroll who was also an avid numerologist. The number is especially present in 'Alice in Wonderland' where it is used several times directly or indirectly. Through the rabbit hole we go?

Michael Casey the cabdriver: Casey is a familiar name in Ireland, meaning in Irish Gaelic, either 'vigilant' or 'watchful.' Casey is the only character in the book who does watch over Rand and guide him in a vigilant manner to safety.

Sligo: Sligo, a gorgeous county in northwest Ireland, is often referred to as 'Yeats Country' a reference to the 20th century Irish poet W.B. Yeats. Yeats, in later years, became as well-known for his dynamic poetry as his obsession with the occult.

The Castle: Little is known of the castle where The Organization works. According to off-hand remarks by Kent St. James, it was constructed in the 12th century and is probably located in the northern part of Austria, possibly within or near the Kalkapen National Park.

Kent St. James: Kent St. James achieved a level of renown while a student at Oxford University in the 1970s with his research on game theory. While still a student, a close friend of his mysteriously died. While no evidence was ever found directly linking

St. James to the murder, he was labeled a suspect and considered an outcast by his contemporaries. After graduation, he disappeared from public record.

-9. The Cavern is located nine levels below the main floor. In "The Inferno" by Dante, there are nine circles of hell.

The Slendoc Meridian. The name, 'Slendoc' is of old Atlantean origin and means, 'sacred,' though it has also been interpreted as 'magic' or 'light-giving.' Multiple studies in linguistics have found no other mention of its name in any language.

Drachen Dining Room: Drachen is German for Dragon. The Dragon is associated with many things mythical, powerful and otherworldly. The name is also intriguing since the number nine in Chinese is associated with the dragon.

Dr. Virgillius: Virgillius is a reference to Virgil who guides Dante through hell in "The Divine Comedy. " There are no public records in relation to Dr. Carmine Virgillius.

Henry Cromwell: The Cromwell name is strong throughout British History. The two most notable being Oliver Cromwell who throughout the mid 17th-century was an English tyrant. His atrocities and genocidal acts to the Irish, in particular, are notorious. Another Cromwell was Thomas Cromwell, advisor to Henry VIII, who helped usher in the age of the English Reformation. Regarding Henry Cromwell:

After graduating from Cambridge with multiple degrees, he earned a reputation for his insight and drive during a 10-year stint in MI-6. He retired from the service before the age of 40, then surfaced occasionally in public roles across the spectrum including the European Union, Icelandic oil claims and other seemingly unrelated ventures. He disappeared from public life in the late 1990s.

Dr. Hope Lightfoot: A native of the American Midwest, she earned her undergraduate degree from Indiana University in English, Music Appreciation and French. She then took a circuitous route studying on fellowships at Julliard, Cambridge and Berklee.

Wolfgang Amadeus Mozart: While his name is synonymous with classical music, many have forgotten how prolific he was composing more than 600 pieces of music in his lifetime. He was also reputed to work furiously under deadline, a trait generally associated with those using the Slendoc Meridian.

The Bear: The identity of The Bear is never established. He might have earned the name either for his bulky size and wild beard or as an allusion to his Russian heritage. At one point, it was believed his last name was Chekov, but it cannot be confirmed

Ich habe die Macht! German for, I have the power! What Weston experiences as he hovers over the found piece of the Slendoc Meridian.

Weston: The scientist who found the piece of the meridian. Weston appears to be a reference to Professor Weston from, "Out of the Silent Planet," and "Perelandra" by C.S. Lewis. The Weston is Lewis's books is a physicist and scientist who spouts doctrines that include moral relativism, science as a god and the teachings of Nietzsche.

Dr. Anne Catherick: Anne Catherick is the name of the woman in white in Wilkie Collins' 'The Woman in White' considered by many critics to be the first mystery novel written.

Conor Renfield: Renfield is a character from 'Dracula' by Bram Stoker. The book – still debated as fiction or historical – features Renfield is a disciple of Dracula before turning on him in the end.

Bearington Heights College. A small liberal arts college in Virginia founded in 1873 as a Methodist College for young men, it established a reputation similar to other colleges its size such as Washington & Lee.

Sine Timore: Latin for 'Without Fear' The Frankish Castle the Organization occupies is inscribed with many ancient sayings. Though the members come from throughout Europe and the castle itself is located in Austria, the common default language in writing appears to be Latin. Sine Timore could be a motto of The Organization or a reminder to separate one's emotion from reason as one ventures into unknown territories inside and outside the mind.

Dr. Dunkel: Dunkel is the German word for 'dark.' There are no other public records on a Dunkel, Dr. Dunkel or the like associated with psychology.

Rand O'Neals parents: We have little record of them here, except what is told to Rand by Dr. Virgillius and Kent St. James. Of course, considering the source of the information, what they told Rand may or may not be true.

Karalveem Valley: An extremely remote area located in the far northeast corner of Russia. Initially used for mining and later for building nuclear power plants, the harsh nature of the environment prevented much contact with the outside world for decades. For example, television was not available to the area's residents until the 1970s and temperatures in the winter can reach 30 below zero.

Mark Wallace Maguire is a writer living south of Atlanta in Red Clay Country. His first book was, "Letters from Red Clay Country: Selected Columns." You can read more about him at www.markwallacemaguire.com